"We're only *supposed*
to be married, Kane!"

"That's what I mean. We can scarcely
have a locked door between us,
especially as we've just reconciled
after a long separation."

Gail started to protest, but Kane
stopped her. "My word is law in this
house, Gail, and you, like everyone
else, will respect it. Do I make myself
clear?"

Furious and unable to curb her
tongue, Gail exploded with, "You're
telling me that you have the right to
give me orders—and that I must obey
them! You seem to have forgotten
what you did to Sandra! If you think
I'm going to risk that, you're wrong!"

"Sandra!" The word was snapped out.
"How dare you mention her! And as for
risks—" disdainfully his glance swept
her figure. "—my girl, you have no
appeal whatsoever for me!"

ANNE HAMPSON

south of capricorn

Harlequin Books

TORONTO • LONDON • LOS ANGELES • AMSTERDAM
SYDNEY • HAMBURG • PARIS • STOCKHOLM • ATHENS • TOKYO

Harlequin Presents edition published June 1982
ISBN 0-373-10507-X

Original hardcover edition published in 1975
by Mills & Boon Limited

CHAPTER ONE

THE two girls stared at one another in consternation, the doctor's words having conveyed their fatal announcement that the mother of Leta was going to die.

'But I can't understand it,' whispered Gail at last. 'She seemed to be recovering satisfactorily.'

The doctor looked at her, his deep-set blue eyes rather sad.

'The will to live has gone, Miss Stafford. Your cousin has several times mentioned the father of her child; she is still in love with him.'

'How can she be!' cut in Dawn angrily. 'He let her down, leaving her with a child – and a wretchedly wild and intractable child at that! Who on earth is going to take on Leta, that's what I'd like to know?'

The doctor shrugged his shoulders.

'The child will be cared for,' was all he said as he picked up his hat from the hall table. 'Good afternoon, Miss Stafford – Miss Atkinson,' and with a slight bow he opened the front door before either girl could do so.

They watched him walk slowly to his car, get in, and drive away. Closing the door, Gail turned to Dawn. Both girls were very close to tears.

'You've been such a good friend to her,' Gail said when, having entered the sitting-room, they sat down, one on the couch, the other in a chair opposite. The room was shabby, with faded carpet and curtains. Sandra Stafford had had a dreadful struggle since the day she was left by the man from the Outback, the tall handsome Australian of whom she often spoke but who was unknown both to Gail and Dawn, both girls having been working abroad at the time of the affair which had such dire results for the girl who had fallen madly in love with the man who, having come over to England to visit relatives, was introduced by one of them to Sandra. Sandra always maintained that a marriage had taken place, but both her cousin and her friend very much doubted this. In fact, Gail was fully convinced that a marriage had not taken place. 'You must be feeling just as shattered as I.'

'I feel I could have helped even more,' returned Dawn sadly, but Gail shook her head.

'We all feel like that at a time like this. But in fairness to ourselves, Dawn, we must claim to have helped – financially, of course. We couldn't help her mentally. She's mentioned the name Kane Farrell several times lately, but I never gained the impression that she was still in love with him.'

'No, she's hidden her feelings very well indeed. I believed, in fact, that she had begun to hate the creature.'

Gail was thoughtful and a small silence reigned for a moment or two. Her grey-green eyes were glinting strangely, but Dawn failed to notice, her thoughts being with the girl in the bed upstairs, the young mother who had lost the will to live – and all because a man had let her down.

'If Sandra only had parents . . .' It was a murmured phrase, for Gail was still absorbed in thought.

'Well, she hasn't – not a relative except you. Leta will have to go into the care of the local authority.'

Gail heaved a sigh, but it was not a sigh of resignation, rather was it an expression of anger, anger against the man from the cattle station who had wrecked her cousin's life.

'Do you know,' she said slowly, looking straight into her friend's eyes, 'I don't see why that cad should get

6

away with it.'

'What do you mean?' frowned Dawn. 'He's already got away with it – as all men do!' she added wrathfully. And, when Gail remained silent, 'If only the kid wasn't such a detestable little brat we might have found a home for her. Joan and Bill have been talking lately about adopting a little girl, but I wouldn't foist that hooligan on my worst enemy.'

'Nor would I,' returned Gail, admitting that her own desire to have the child was nil. Had Leta been a nice child then Gail's parents might have agreed to give her a home, but the child was bad-tempered and rude; she was totally immune to authority or to any sympathetic approach. It was as if she resented anyone telling her what to do or what not to do. 'She obviously takes after her father, for I'm sure she didn't inherit all those vices from her mother.'

'She did not,' with force from Dawn. 'Sandra was the sweetest, most likeable girl in the world . . .' Dawn trailed off; both girls gave a small shudder even before she added, 'Oh God, I'm talking as if she's gone already!'

'Let's go up.' Gail spoke rather shortly, but only because the thought was on her mind that soon they would not be able to go up and spend time with Leta's mother. 'She might not be awake, but we'll see.'

'She was ready to doze when the doctor was here.' But Dawn rose from the chair all the same, and accompanied Gail up to Sandra's bedroom. It was shabby like the room below, and the curtains were partly drawn together so that a dimness pervaded the small apartment, adding to the air of gloom which both girls had previously experienced, and commented upon, little knowing how much cause there was shortly going to be for that gloom.

'She's asleep . . .' Gail paused, her heart jerking. '*Is*

7

she asleep . . . or . . .?'

Dawn swallowed hard.

'She must be. She can't — I mean, it's only ten minutes since the doctor left.'

Sandra opened her eyes and both girls gave a small sigh of relief.

'You're there.' Her voice trailed weakly. 'Come over to the bed. I want to talk to you both.'

'Sandra dear, you must think of nothing else except getting better,' began Gail, sitting down on the edge of the bed and taking hold of her cousin's hand. 'Think of Leta—'

'She's caused me so much trouble. Is there such another in the whole world, do you think?'

'She's naughty, yes, but not wicked—'

'Gail, you're always so honest. You know very well that my daughter is not only wicked, but actually evil.'

'Sandra!' exclaimed Dawn, speaking too loudly altogether. 'No child of four could be evil. It's just that she hasn't had a man to keep her in order. You've spoiled her, you must admit that?'

'Yes, perhaps I have,' owned Sandra in the same weak tone of voice. 'But many children are spoiled, and they don't turn out like my Leta.'

Neither Dawn nor Gail could say anything to this. For it was the truth that Leta was just about the most detestable child possible. No one liked her; she rarely received so much as a smile from the other people living in the small terrace in which Sandra's rented cottage was situated. In fact, the neighbours had all forbidden their children to play with her, so appalling were her manners and so vicious her temper.

'Are you wanting to sleep?' asked Dawn, noting the drooping of Sandra's eyelids. 'Shall we leave you, darling?'

8

Sandra shook her head.

'I want . . .' She looked wide awake all at once and a firmness had entered her voice, 'I want Leta to be taken to her father.'

'Taken to her—?' Dawn stared, then opened her mouth to say something which would surely reveal the fact of the doctor's informing them that there was no hope of Sandra's recovery, but she was stopped by a warning glance from Gail.

'But, dear,' Gail murmured soothingly, 'you yourself are quite capable of taking care of Leta. And you dearly love her, despite her shortcomings.'

'Gail—' Sandra looked deeply into her eyes, 'I've only just a moment ago remarked on your honesty. But you're not being honest now. I am not going to live. I have no desire to do so. But I want my child to have a home. My husband is a wealthy grazier – a very wealthy grazier. I want Leta to go and live with him.'

Silence. Gail was thinking of the legacy which she and Sandra had shared, over a year ago. Her own share of the money was there, sufficient for her fare . . . And why, she said again, should Kane Farrell get away with it?

Dawn was still staring, but looking rather helpless at the same time. She transferred her gaze to Gail, saw the glint in those grey-green eyes and wondered greatly at it.

Suddenly there was a deafening clamour coming from the room below and Dawn rose at once from the chair she was occupying.

'I'll go down to Leta,' she offered, and Gail sensed the element of relief Dawn experienced at being able to escape from this conversation. 'She's just arrived home from play-school.'

The door soon closed behind Dawn and for a long

moment there was silence in the room. Then Sandra spoke, telling Gail that her share of the legacy was intact. Staring in surprise, Gail said that she had expected it would all have been spent by now.

'I've saved it, knowing that I would want it – for the purpose I mentioned. I did think at one time that I might, when the time came, have to employ someone to take her to her father. However, you mentioned yesterday that you have due to you a month's leave, as you've not had one for so long.' Sandra paused, frowning a little as if she were either in pain or feeling very tired. But her voice had been steady all the time and it was still steady as she went on to explain that the money from the legacy was just about enough for the fares of both Gail and Leta.

Gail listened without interruption, her mind on the fact that she herself had never believed in a marriage ever having taken place. The fact that Sandra was so confidently talking about sending Leta to her father produced in Gail some doubts about her own conviction, and for the first time she did begin to wonder if Sandra had spoken the truth when she maintained, right at the beginning, that she was married to Kane Farrell. But, thought Gail frowning in some puzzlement, if that were the case, why then had Sandra not tried to get some money from this wealthy grazier? And why had she never used his name? She had never used it for Leta either.

However, whether or not a marriage had taken place Gail was still of the opinion that the man in the case should not be allowed to get away with it, and this she strongly put forward later when her mother protested at her intention of carrying out Sandra's wishes and taking Leta to her father.

'He's the father, and whether married or not to Leta's mother he should be made to accept the responsibility now that the child has no one else willing to take her. I'm going to do as Sandra wished, Mother, and no amount of argument will prevent me. In any case, it's a matter of honour, because I promised Sandra I would do as she asked.'

Her mother shook her head resignedly.

'You've always had a strong will, dear,' she said with a small sigh. 'So I expect you'll do what you think is right. However, you must let me warn you that this Kane Farrell will in all probability send you packing with Leta. After all, as they never married he has no legal responsibility for the child.'

'Sandra has always maintained that they were married.' Gail spoke automatically, her mind on the fact that neither a marriage certificate nor Leta's birth certificate had been found among her cousin's belongings. They could have been destroyed, she supposed, but they were not the kind of documents a woman did destroy. On the contrary, they were usually safely guarded.

'I don't believe it. It's natural that she would say that, because of the disgrace, as it were. But—' Mrs. Stafford shook her head, 'I'm not convinced, Gail, and won't be until you return and tell me that the man really was married to poor Sandra.'

'I wonder what he looks like?' mused Gail, veering the matter a little. 'Sandra never could be persuaded to show either Dawn or me a photograph.'

'You didn't find one in her belongings?'

Gail shook her head, the tears starting to her eyes as she recalled the unhappy task of sorting out her cousin's pitiful little store of possessions.

'She described him,' she said after a while. 'He's certainly the tough handsome type of giant one associates with the Outback graziers. He owns a cattle station of ten thousand square miles, so Sandra told me one day when she was talking about him. He inherited it from his father, apparently.'

'What else did she tell you?'

'Very little, really,' frowned Gail reflectively. 'But somehow I gained the impression that the man was a boaster.'

It was her mother's turn to frown.

'You mean, he might not be all he described himself to be?'

'I don't know . . .' A pause and then, 'I'm pretty sure he is as wealthy as she says – no, don't ask me why I have this conviction, because I don't know myself. What I meant about his boasting was that he seems to have talked far too much about his possessions. Wealthy people don't normally go on about what they own. This Kane Farrell seems to have done just this.'

'Sandra said so?'

'No, she never actually said it. I gained the impression, as I've said, yet I can't explain why I should have gained it.'

'And you're firmly set on going to Australia?' her mother said after a while. 'You're going to appear pretty foolish when he tells you to clear off and take Leta with you.'

The glint entered her daughter's eyes.

'I shall leave her – dump her on him!'

Her mother grimaced.

'Knowing you as I do,' she said, shaking her head, 'I can accept that. My, what an absorbing scene it will be when you turn up and say, "Mr. Farrell, here is your child." '

Gail smiled at the mental picture that arose before her.

'He's going to feel pretty sick, I must admit. Serve him right! Perhaps he'll think twice about seducing another young girl.'

'Has the thought that he might be married ever entered your mind?'

'Of course. But what difference will that make? His wife can look to the child.'

'And what an experience that will be!'

'Leta'll disrupt everything in less than ten minutes.'

'No doubt at all about that,' was the grim rejoinder from Mrs. Stafford. But she did then go on to reassert her own conviction that Leta would never find a home at the cattle station owned by her father. 'Do, dear, consider a little more before you go out there,' she added, but saw at once by that familiar glint that her daughter's mind was immovably made up.

'Where's the brat now?' Gail was asking a few minutes later. 'She should have been home a quarter of an hour ago.'

'She won't stay with Mrs. Goring, who is so kind as to offer to bring her home. I expect she's playing in a gutter somewhere, or beating up some other little girl.'

'Bad-tempered wretch! How on earth did Sandra produce a child like Leta?'

'It seems impossible,' agreed Mrs. Stafford, shaking her head. 'She was such a darling child herself when she was little. I didn't see much of her, of course, because as you know I couldn't get on with her mother. I believe it was this that made Sandra so independent as far as I was concerned. She wouldn't allow me to give her a thing.'

'You gave it through me, though.' Gail paused a moment. She was musing on her own attitude towards Leta, who as a baby was so very attractive. But from the moment she could think for herself she had been almost uncontrollable. She would lie on the floor and scream if she could not have all her own way; she would think nothing of grasping a handful of hair and pulling it if some other little girl did anything to annoy her. At play-school she was disliked, but the woman running it had taken pity on Sandra when she heard that, were it not for Leta, she could take a part-time job, so earning a little extra money for herself and the child. 'You know, Mother, I sometimes think that she can't be as bad as she appears. After all, she's only four.'

'Four and a half. And don't forget, badness comes out at a very early age. She's bad all right, and the best place for her is with her father — annoying him and making a little hell of his life. But I'm sure he won't have her, especially when he knows what she's like.'

'He won't have time to discover what she's like,' was Gail's grim reply. 'I shall simply dump her on him, as I've said.'

'She might begin right away — spit at him or some such thing.'

'She won't. You don't know Leta as well as I. She can be bribed.'

Her mother threw up her hands.

'Another vice!' she exclaimed.

'Yes, she has them all. You name it and Leta has it. Lord, it makes you wonder if it's safe to bring children into the world!'

Mrs. Stafford had to laugh at this.

'You'll never produce a child like Leta,' she told her with conviction. And for a quiet moment she gazed at her daughter, taking in the fine and noble lines of her face, a face of character and determination. And yet the full wide mouth was soft and Mrs. Stafford smiled faintly on recalling all those incidents when Gail had given forth compassion in abundance, whenever it happened to be called for. The eyes, of so unusual but attractive a colour, were large and widely-spaced beneath a high intelligent forehead. The dark brown hair with its bronze glints was long and silky and luxuriously thick. High cheekbones, attractive though they were, seemed not to fit in with the short nose and pointed chin. And yet it was an extraordinarily beautiful face and one that invariably brought the light of admiration to the eyes of the men with whom Gail came into contact both in her working and her social life. Mrs. Stafford was justifiably proud of her only child, just as Gail was proud of her pretty mother, with her slender figure and happy carefree way of life. Her husband was just as attractive, in a different way of course, and always Gail had thanked the stars for her having the kind of parents whose affection and understanding had gone such a long way in preventing any dissension whatsoever between them and their daughter.

It was less than a fortnight later that Gail set forth, with Leta, for the cattle station known as Vernay Downs, situated in the Never-Never, just south of Capricorn. The child was dressed in denims and a bright red cotton sweater; on her head she wore a bright green knitted cap with a red bobble on top and over her shoulder she carried a red leather bag containing sweets and chocolate, and a toothbrush in a waterproof case. Gail's mother had provided the entire outfit plus the contents of the shoulder-bag. Not one word of thanks had left the child's lips. She had told Gail that the toothbrush would never be used.

'I don't like cleaning my teeth, so Mummy never made me,' she said.

'Nevertheless, you'll clean your teeth whenever the opportunity presents itself,' Gail told her. 'You're not to eat sweets without cleaning your teeth afterwards.'

'You can't always clean them. What about in the taxi?' Leta had said when, all the luggage having been placed in the hall, they were waiting, with Gail's parents, for the cab to arrive.

'You mustn't eat your sweets yet,' said Mr. Stafford mildly. 'You've only just had your breakfast.'

'I'll please myself,' returned Leta, stamping on the floor to give emphasis to her words. 'If I want to eat my sweets I shall eat them.' At which Mr. Stafford looked across at his daughter and silently conveyed to her his anxiety about the journey over to Australia.

'You've taken on more than you can chew,' he managed to get in when Leta, having seen a small insect crawling along the path, went forth to put her foot on it. 'What a horror! No wonder her mother gave up; I'd do so myself if I had a child like that.'

'Paul,' protested his wife, 'you shouldn't say such things. You know how any reference to poor Sandra makes our daughter sad.'

'I'm sorry,' he muttered, then lapsed into silence, breaking it only on the arrival of the taxi when he gave the driver the necessary instructions for getting them to the airport. Once there another silence followed, with both Mr. and Mrs. Stafford sending worried glances at each other, and at their daughter.

'I can manage her,' Gail told them confidently, noting this anxiety. 'You'll remember, Mother, that I told you she can be bribed.'

'Why have to bribe a child?' was the indignant query. 'It's disgraceful! Sandra, poor dear child, must have had a dreadful time with her.'

'Undoubtedly,' murmured her husband. 'Were she mine I'd flay her alive!'

'She certainly needs controlling.'

'Her father is shortly to have the task,' said Gail grimly. 'And the best of luck to him!'

There were a few tears on Mrs. Stafford's cheeks when at length the good-byes were being said, and Gail, herself deeply affected but managing to hold back the tears, reminded her mother that she would in all probability be back within a fortnight.

'I wish it were a shorter period, dear,' sighed her mother. 'Can't you manage it in a week?'

Gail shook her head, saying that the journey following the flight itself would be a very long one.

'I shall have to hire a car, or something. There's an Overlanding bus, I've been told by the girl in the travel agency, but I've enough money to hire a car.'

Her father glanced at Leta, who was deliberately pulling threads out of the new knitted gloves she had taken from her hands.

'I am of the opinion,' he remarked significantly, 'that it will be preferable – and certainly less wearing on your nerves, my dear – to taking that young brat on a public conveyance, especially for as many hours as that.'

'I agree wholeheartedly,' said Mrs. Stafford, handkerchief held to her face. 'Darling, do be careful!'

Gail had to smile.

'There's no danger, pet,' she said soothingly as she put an arm around her mother's shoulders. 'Anyone would think I was taking a load of explosives to Australia!'

At this her father sent another glance at the small child who was now scraping the shiny toe of one shoe with the sole of the other, determined to take the gloss off completely.

'I'd feel rather less apprehensive if you were,' he rejoined with a crisp sort of chill in his voice which neither his wife nor his daughter had ever heard before. 'That, over there, is more destructive than any load of dynamite!'

'What's dynamite?' inquired Leta, suddenly interested in the grown-ups.

'Something that explodes – blows you up!'

'Ooh . . . I'd like to blow somebody up!'

'And kill them?' Mr. Stafford was frowning heavily, but Leta was totally undaunted by this.

'Of course.'

'Come along,' snapped Mrs. Stafford. 'Take hold of Gail's hand! If you're not careful the aeroplane will go without you!'

'I don't want it to!' Leta exclaimed, running to take the proffered hand. 'I'm going to live with my daddy!' And to the utter amazement of Gail and her parents Leta's eyes took on a glow of excitement which transformed her whole appearance.

'She really wants to go!' Mrs. Stafford looked bewilderedly at her daughter. Gail could only shake her head, recalling how, since the first mention of the father with whom she was now going to live, Leta had retired completely into herself, showing emotion only when she had one of her tantrums. Not a tear had been shed when she was told that she would not see her mother again and, troubled by the child's long silences, Mrs. Stafford had sent for the doctor. It was he who told Leta that, if she did not go to her father, then she would have to live in a children's home. Gail was furious about his, but the doctor did manage to convince her, after a while, that some threat was necessary in order to make the child go quietly, as it were.

'Unless she is willing you'll never get her on that plane,' he had warned, and as he had the support of both her parents Gail at last forgave him for the ultimatum he had offered the child. For it was an undisputable fact that, if Leta made up her mind not to board the plane, then she would fight like a tiger to obtain her own way. Gail certainly did not relish a scene where Leta, lying on the ground, would scream and kick and eventually have to be dragged or carried to the plane.

The threat having done what it was intended to do, Leta became resigned to the idea of living with her father. But apart from one occasion when she had said, quite unexpectedly, 'I hope my daddy's nice,' she had not until this moment displayed an atom of enthusiasm, and Gail had surmised that, as far as the child's reaction was concerned, living with her father was the lesser of the two evils.

'Are you really looking forward to seeing your daddy?' asked Mr. Stafford, and Leta nodded her head.

'I want to see what he's like. If he's nice then I'll be a good girl for him!'

This left no impression on Gail. She knew Leta far too well to take any notice of a promise like that.

'Good-bye, darling.' It was the last time this was to be said, and mother and daughter had one final hug. Leta was again engaged in mutilating her shoe, but soon Gail had her firmly by the hand, and it was not until they were on the plane that she let go.

'You've pinched my fingers! I hate you!' Leta stamped her foot, glaring at Gail. 'You'd no need to hold my hand so hard, because I wouldn't have run away!' Gail said nothing. She had held on simply because she was not taking any chances. Knowing Leta as she did, she was quite prepared for trouble, even though the way had been paved by the doctor's words, and even by Leta's enthusiasm. However, it were better always to be prepared for the worst with a child of Leta's temperament – a temperament of changing mood and heightened passions. 'I'll pinch *you* if you do it again! You've no right—'

'Sit down and be quiet!' snapped Gail at last, acutely aware of the surprised and disapproving stares of other passengers.

'I won't! I'm going to stand up all the way – so there!'

A rather stout gentleman with heavy moustaches and protuberant eyes, noticing the scene as he made to take a seat opposite, looked down at Leta and said sternly,

'Do as your mother tells you, young lady! Sit down at once! You're a very naughty little girl! No, don't you dare to interrupt me! My word, but you want a good smacking. Do as I tell you – sit down beside your mother and be quiet!'

Stunned for one disbelieving moment, Leta then did no less than kick out at the man, catching him just below the knee.

'Leta!' exclaimed Gail, horrified and fervently thankful that her parents could not witness this scene. 'You naughty girl! Say you're sorry, at once!'

But this was too much to expect. Instead of the apology the man received a pettish, 'Mind your own business!' before Leta put out her tongue at him. For the rest of the flight he spoke neither to Leta nor to Gail, but his glances at Gail from time to time left her in no doubt at all of his opinion of her as a 'mother'. She would have liked to disillusion him, just for her own comfort, but she refrained, deciding that it did not matter much what he thought of her, seeing that she and he would never meet again.

At Brisbane Gail and Leta changed to a train and to her relief Leta fell asleep and from then on Gail could read her book in peace. However, after reading for a while she became interested in the scenery as the train travelled through the highlands of the Great Divide into the area of brigalow scrub and sub-tropical woodlands. The sun began to sink, but there was still some time to go before the brief twilight fell.

The twilight would last about twenty minutes, Gail had been told, and after that darkness would descend rapidly. And it was almost dark before the train drew into the station and Gail felt rather apprehensive on noticing that there was very little sign of civilization. For example, there was no real town; certainly there was no sign that cars could be hired. Suddenly aware of her failure to make the appropriate inquiries when in Brisbane, she approached a railway official and explained what she required. His eyes opened wide before he shook his head, scratching it meanwhile and appearing to think he had met a madwoman.

'There's no car here,' he informed her at last. 'Not one to hire, that is. Why, a car could be waiting here for a twelvemonth for someone to come along and want it. No, miss, you'll have to wait for the Overlander.'

'When is that?'

'What's the Overlander?' piped up Leta who, having been wakened from her sleep, was not in the best of moods. 'I want a taxi, so you'd better get one! Gail, get a taxi!'

Ignoring her, Gail turned again to the man, repeating her question. The Overlander would not be here that night, she was told.

'Then where can we stay? Is there an hotel?' She asked the question automatically, even though a glance around had told her that this was no place where visitors would be found. It was merely a stopping off place where the passengers would be met by relatives or someone else who happened to be expecting them. A couple had just entered a big overlanding car which was covered with yellow dust and carrying on its bumpers several canvas water bags; Gail watched as the car moved away. Another one was waiting, but no one came towards it. The train moved and gathered speed while the driver of the car stood by the door and watched it, a deep frown on his bronzed and furrowed brow.

'There's no hotel,' the railway official was saying, his interest now with the man by the stationary car, rather than with Gail and her problems.

'But—'

'Your people not arrived?' interrupted the official, calling to the man.

'I can't think what's happened.'

'How far have you come?' Although he had put the question, the official was already moving away.

'From Vernay Downs,' replied the man, and quite naturally Gail's heart gave a little jerk.

'Vernay Downs?' she repeated rather hastily, as if afraid the man would enter the car and drive away. 'I'm going there!' What unbelievable good luck, she was telling herself, not stopping to think of the difficulties that must inevitably follow in the wake of her impulsiveness. 'Could you take us, please?'

The man frowned and strode towards her, his eyes running over her and taking in her travel-stained appearance.

'You're going to Vernay Downs?' He sounded incredulous, she thought. 'Are you expected?' His tone said quite clearly that she was *not* expected.

'No, I'm not expected.' Already she knew a tinge of uneasiness, but this in no way lessened her determination to get a lift. 'I've brought something very important for a Mr. Kane Farrell.'

The man's puzzlement increased.

'Kane Farrell?' Again his eyes ran over her, and then he looked at Leta, who at this moment was endeavouring to stuff a whole bar of chocolate into her mouth.

'Something very important – and yet you're not expected?'

She coloured slightly, her uneasiness increasing.

'I'm afraid I can't explain,' she said apologetically. 'I mean, I can't tell you what it is that I've brought.'

'It's me,' interposed Leta, both cheeks bulging with the chocolate inside them. 'That's what it is!'

The man then produced a weak sort of grin before returning his attention to Gail.

'Do you really mean to say that you didn't let the Boss know you were coming?' he asked with a bewildered shake of his head. 'How did you expect to get from here to Vernay Downs?'

Ignoring his second question, she said,

'The Boss? Do you work for Mr. Farrell?'

'That's right. Cattleman – stockrider. Ever heard of them?' His sentences were drawled out, yet short. His hands, half tucked into the pockets of his slim-fitting denims, were as brown as his face; and Gail wondered if he typified the men out here. Toughened by the weather, he certainly looked the part of the outdoor man whose task it was to look after the cattle, out in the wide open spaces.

'Yes, I've heard of stockriders,' answered Gail. 'But you're the first one I've met.'

He held out his hand, introducing himself as he did so.

'Dave Campbell – at your service.'

'I'm Gail Stafford, and this is Leta.'

'Your daughter?'

Gail shook her head, and after a slight hesitation he asked if she were married. She said no, then ventured to inquire if Kane Farrell was married. No, returned Dave, adding that Kane Farrell lived only for his work. Gail felt a prickle of nerves as she heard a murmured, 'Kane Farrell,' coming from beside the car.

23

'I've come all the way from England to live with my daddy—' broke in Leta, and Gail said swiftly, noting apprehensively that Dave's eyes had widened in an interrogating stare,

'Leta dear, please don't interrupt when we're speaking. In that suitcase over there — the small one — you'll find another bar of chocolate.'

'Will I?' Sheer wickedness looked out from those bright blue eyes — eyes vivid and large and so inordinately attractive at times. Yet for the most part of the time they might have been the eyes of some she-devil, such wicked glints did they possess. 'I'll get it, then,' and off she went, carrying an air of triumph which made Gail wonder how her father would deal with her. Would he be strong enough to master the wretched child? But that was his problem, or would be soon, she thought, not without a great deal of satisfaction. There he was, sublimely unaware of what was coming to him, the man who believed he had got away with his dastardly treatment of poor Sandra. It was not as if he didn't know about his daughter. Sandra had written to him twice, informing him of Leta's existence. Both letters had been ignored. Would he suffer any pangs of remorse when the fact of Sandra's death was made known to him? Gail thought not, since he must be a man totally devoid of feeling not to have given some sort of help to the girl he had treated so badly.

'You didn't answer my question about your getting from here to Vernay Downs,' Dave was saying, having, to Gail's infinite relief, once again taken no notice of what Leta had said. 'Supposing I hadn't happened to be here?'

'I thought I could have hired a car.'

At this his eyes opened wider than ever.

'You did!' he exclaimed. 'Here?' He spread a hand and she once again took in the dusty station with its

24

primitive platform, the single shed that constituted the station 'buildings', the utter loneliness of the place. 'You weren't very well advised, obviously.' The merest pause and then he added, 'Well, your luck happens to be in. Little girl,' he said to Leta, 'you take the back seat—'

'I want the front seat!'

This was sheer awkwardness and Gail, overwhelmingly grateful to the man Dave, could have shaken her till she cried. However, she wasn't even given the chance to speak as Dave, after the first start of surprise, said firmly and authoritatively,

'Leta, get into the back of the car.'

'I—'

'Because if you don't, then you won't go in it at all!'

The child's face swelled as air was allowed to fill her cheeks. She turned purple with temper and Gail found herself apologizing. But Dave intervened, with another warning, and after a struggle within herself, Leta capitulated.

'Good gracious!' exclaimed Gail without thinking. 'You've won!'

Dave looked oddly at her.

'It's a damned funny business,' he said, and it was as if he were having the greatest struggle not to ask questions of her. But he managed to control his curiosity as he proceeded to put the luggage into the boot of the car. The porter came out and offered help; he looked relieved, and it was not difficult for Gail to guess that he had been worried about having a woman and child on his hands until the arrival of the Overlander.

'Well, we're off!' Dave said good-bye to the porter and soon the car was leaving the station. 'I expect you know we've a very long way to go?'

'Yes, I do know that.'

'We'll make camp quite soon. I've driven a long distance today already and I don't feel like driving in the dark.'

'Make camp?' came the voice from the back seat. 'Is that camping?' and when Dave said yes, it was, Leta continued, 'I'm not camping—' She stopped, swallowing, as her mouth was full of chocolate. 'My teacher went camping and she got bitten by scorpions.'

'You'll not be bitten by scorpions, little girl,' Dave assured her soothingly. 'In fact, you'll enjoy camping. It can be fun. I loved it when I was a kid like you.'

'I'm not a kid!'

'Touchy, isn't she?' Dave was driving fast and his attention was on the road. 'Some relative of yours?'

'My dead cousin's child.'

'You had to bring her with you?' It was obvious that already Dave was wondering how anyone in her right mind would bring a child like Leta with her.

'I had to, yes.'

'I'm extraordinarily fond of kids as a rule—' He stopped, aware of his indiscretion, but in any case Leta was soon in with,

'You like children, but you don't like me?'

'Little girl—'

'I don't like you, so there! I don't like anybody! I might not like my daddy—'

'Leta!' interrupted Gail, but Leta continued,

'I promised to call him Daddy, and say what Gail told me to say—'

'Be quiet, Leta!'

'—because she's giving me chocolate and lots of things, but I don't know if I will like him—'

'I said be quiet!' Gail was red in the face, wondering what Dave was thinking about all this, and what conclusions he was coming to. 'That's enough! Any more and you won't get the chocolate, or anything else!'

'Not get it? Then I won't say the things you've told me to. I won't say, "Hello, Daddy," so there!'

Dave turned his head and slanted a glance at Gail.

'Funny business,' he muttered again, and then lapsed into silence. But he seemed deep in thought ... and Gail wished that she had the power to read those thoughts. However, there was one thing she was thankful for: Leta had not mentioned who her father was.

CHAPTER TWO

'THAT's the Southern Cross.' Dave spoke as he took the car off the Bitumen and on to a bumpy road which led to the banks of a creek. 'It's a wonderful sight, eh?'

'Beautiful.' Awed the tone as Gail took it all in, the night sky over this vast land, the stars and the moon, the indistinct outlines of various rises in the land, rises which helped a little to relieve the monotony of these apparently endless plains.

'We'll make camp here.' Dave stopped and got out, with Gail following. Leta said she was staying where she was.

'Don't you want anything to eat?' asked Dave in surprise.

'I've got some chocolate. Shut the door, I'm cold!'

Gail apologized and said that Leta was tired. Dave, though frowning, agreed and, obeying Leta's second and more imperious command, he closed the car door.

'The camping gear's in the back. If you'd collect some dry wood we can make a fire.'

Gail did as she was told, watching Dave out of the corner of her eye as she went about picking up small dead branches which lay on the ground close to the dry creek bed. Dave was tall and strong, the kind of man she had always admired. He was quiet, working with speed as he made camp. Leta watched from the car; she slowly became a shadow behind a window as Gail moved away into the darkness of an Australian night. But as the fire got under way the glow lit up an area all around and Leta in the car became a figure encased in fiery red – like Satan's cub, Dawn would have said, for

28

Dawn had the most vivid imagination of anyone whom Gail had ever met. Satan's cub clothed in fire.

Gail wanted to speak to her, so she watched Dave as he busied himself, waiting for him to move farther away from the car. She had no wish that what she had to say to Leta should be overheard. At length the opportunity came and Gail went swiftly over and opened the car door.

'I'm cold!' shouted Leta angrily. 'What do you want?'

'Be quiet!' Gail turned and looked with slight apprehension towards the place where Dave was working. He had glanced up on hearing the angry voice, but apparently he was not interested, for he bent again to his task. 'I have something to say to you. Listen, Leta! You mustn't talk to Dave, do you hear?'

'Why not?'

'Because I don't want him to know why we've come to this place. Don't say anything about your daddy—'

'I've already said something about him!'

'Dave didn't take much notice — well, I hope he didn't begin thinking too much about your chatterings,' she amended, recalling his remarking that it was a funny business. If only Leta weren't so highly intelligent, thought Gail, then it would be far easier to get her co-operation, to cajole her even. But she *was* highly intelligent and in consequence she was often able to see through people.

'Why don't you want him to know why we've come to this place?'

'Because it isn't any of his business. It's a private matter between you and me and your new daddy.'

'What will you give me if I don't talk about my daddy?' The child's gaze was wickedly avaricious. 'I want some new clothes for my doll.'

'You've already torn two sets up—'

'I didn't like them! I want some better ones!'

'I can't get you dolls' clothes here, Leta,' said Gail rather desperately. 'What else will you have?'

'Nothing. I'm going to talk about my daddy. I'm going to say that he left my mummy on her own to look after me. I know he did, because I heard you talking to your mummy and daddy about it, one day when you didn't know I was listening. It was when I was staying with you, after Mummy went away to heaven.'

'Leta, you mustn't say things like that in front of Dave! Your daddy won't like it at all if Dave knows, because, you see, Dave works for him—'

'I want two dresses and a coat, and some underclothes!'

Gail gave a wrathful sigh.

'I've just said I can't get dolls' clothes in this place.'

'There'll be some shops at the town where Daddy lives.'

'He lives on a big farm – oh, Leta, I've already told you about his home and the cows and everything!'

'If there's a shop will you buy me some clothes for my doll?' Still the wicked gleam in the lovely eyes. And the little rosebud mouth was actually curved in a sneer.

'Yes – yes, of course I will.'

'All right. I won't talk to Dave about my daddy.'

Wretched creature! How, Gail asked herself once again, had a girl as sweet-natured as Sandra given birth to a fiendish child like Leta?

'That's a good girl,' returned Gail, feeling more like slapping Leta's legs hard than speaking in this manner to her.

Leta laughed.

'I'm not a good girl at all! I'm naughty and you

don't like me! Nobody likes me because I scream and kick and shout at people.'

Another sigh escaped Gail. She had no intention of prolonging this conversation and she merely reminded Leta that, should she as much as mention her daddy or her mummy, then she would not get the clothes for her doll. Not that the clothes would do her any good, decided Gail as she moved away after closing the car door. Leta would very soon have them in shreds – or even take a pair of scissors and cut them up. However, that was unimportant; the important thing was that the offer of a bribe was going to put a brake on the child's tongue. What was she going to be like when she grew up? Gail shuddered and mentally expressed the hope that she would remain a spinster – for if she didn't then some poor man's life was going to be ruined. Gail turned, then stopped, amazed at what she saw. Leta was against the car window, her head resting on her hands ... and she seemed to be sobbing, for her shoulders heaved. Hesitating in indecision, Gail turned again and continued on her way, convinced that, should she turn back, Leta would subject her to a burst of vicious anger.

But Gail was worried; she felt, for the first time, that the child's trouble could be psychological. Was it the fact of having no proper home life, of having no father, that had caused the child to be what she was? Gail had always owned that Leta was a lonely child; she was bound to be lonely, when other children were forbidden by their parents to play with her. Highly intelligent as she was, Leta must have gradually become aware of being different from other children in that she had only one parent. This, plus the fact of her loneliness, could have affected the child in such a way as to have changed her character completely. Gail with a backswitch of memory recalled the time when Leta was as adorable a baby, and toddler, as any other child she had known. Something had gone wrong; Sandra might not have given her the attention she should and, as the child became more and more intractable, Sandra did, Gail knew, give up hope. She made no pretence about Leta, not to anyone, admitting that the child was not merely naughty but wicked. Musing in this way, Gail wished she could like the child just a little, but it was impossible; no one could like her, and had she been Gail's own daughter she would undoubtedly have given up hope, just as Sandra did, of ever bringing about a change in the child's character.

After the meal was over Dave cleared away, helped by Gail who washed the dishes while he gathered gum leaves with which to line the hollows he had already dug out of the earth. Mats were brought to cover the gum leaves, and rugs for covering, for, said Dave, the night would be cold. All this could have been fun had she known Dave better, she thought, but he was after all still a stranger and she was still rather shy with him, being quieter than she normally would have been. She wanted to know a lot about Kane Farrell, but had not the courage to ask questions which might be resented by Dave whose loyalty was obvious. The Boss, as he had called Kane Farrell, was someone to be respected, and for that reason Dave might well tell Gail outright that he could not answer questions. Perhaps tomorrow they would have become more used to one another; he might himself vouchsafe information about his employer.

She was right. He did offer information, as they raced along the Bitumen, having started out at first light after breaking camp. This was to Gail an interesting operation and she watched attentively as Dave stamped out the embers and then covered them with earth. He examined the kit to see that nothing had been left behind and then, having assured himself that nothing had been left undone, slid into the drive seat and turned the car towards the Bitumen.

'A strange man at times, the Boss,' mused Dave after the subject of the man had already been broached. 'He lives for his work. Life for him is in the saddle. Of course, it's not surprising that he keeps away from the homestead as much as is possible, what with his stepmother and her daughter. Mind you, the daughter's a smasher if ever there was one! And she'd snare him if she could. Maybe she'll succeed one day, and then Kane and his stepmother might get along a little better.'

'Does his stepmother own part of the ranch – er – the station, I mean?'

'Not an inch of land. But she can stay in the house for as long as she likes. That's what the trouble is. She tries to run the place and Kane just won't have it. She's the mistress, she insists, and of course this is so – until Kane marries, which I'm afraid he never will do.'

'He's a woman-hater?' This was said in a curious tone, Gail having merely voiced it in order to gain more information, for she had proof that he was not a woman-hater.

'I wouldn't go as far as that. It's just that he doesn't seem to be interested enough to want anything serious to develop between him and any woman. We have our various entertainments here, such as the shed dances and film shows, and of course the parties, and he meets the ambitious females all the time. But he limits his interest to being polite, and his activities with the opposite sex to dancing.'

'I see . . .' It wasn't always like that, reflected Gail grimly. 'He's changed, apparently—' She stopped, automatically putting a hand to her mouth as she realized what she had said. Dave slanted her a swift look of inquiry, and no wonder, she thought. He must be becoming extremely curious already, without her saying things which must surely increase that curiosity.

'Changed?' he repeated. 'I don't understand? You mentioned yesterday that you hadn't met Kane – when we were talking about him, remember?'

'Of course. And it's quite true that we've never met.'

'And yet you say he's changed.'

She bit her lip, wondering what to say.

'I had heard that he – er – liked the women.'

'You had?' Dave's eyes opened very wide. 'Now who could have told you a thing like that?'

'I – er – just heard it somewhere,' she replied lamely. 'Mr. Farrell came over to England for a visit, a few years ago.'

'Did he? I wouldn't know; I wasn't working for him at that time.' Dave increased his speed and to Gail's relief seemed totally absorbed in his driving. No more was said about Kane for a long time. But Leta chatted, declaring that the place was strange, without people or buildings. She wanted to know the reason for this and Dave tried to explain.

'I don't like it when there's no houses and shops,' she said with a pout. 'I want to go home!'

Gail was guarded, and spoke soothingly to the child, anxiously hoping that she would remember her promise and not say anything which would provide Dave with any real clue as to why they had come to Australia. They were now driving through the vast region of tropical savanna where scrub and eucalyptus prevailed. It was lonely bushland of the interior, wild untamed land, awesome in its silence and its total lack of human habitation. On the skyline appeared a range of mountains, headlands of a shoreline which existed millions of years ago when an inland sea occupied the area in which Dave was driving.

After a long while he began speaking to Gail again and she learned a little more of the friction existing in the household of the man to whom she was taking Leta, the man she hated even though she had never yet set eyes on him. Mrs. Farrell, Kane's stepmother, had been offered a new home by Kane, but she had refused to budge from the home to which his father had brought her two years previously. He had died after less than a year of marriage and ever since then there had been almost continuous quarrels between Kane and his stepmother.

'The daughter,' put in Gail, feeling she should say something, 'she also lives in the house?'

'She came last year, ostensibly to comfort her mother, but more like it was with the intention of landing herself a rich grazier. Kane's her choice, but as I said, he isn't at all interested. Although,' he added after a thoughtful pause, 'he might at some time decide that marriage to Ertha would solve his problems regarding his stepmother. She might pull in her horns once her own daughter is mistress at Vernay Downs.'

How, wondered Gail not without malice, were they all going to fare once the little fiend Leta was installed? For installed she certainly was going to be since Gail was determined not to take her back to England. Was Kane Farrell free to marry this Ertha? Gail wished she could have been sure that he had married Sandra, but unfortunately she was still of the same mind about that. It was most unlikely that a marriage had taken place. As she had always maintained, if Sandra were Kane Farrell's wife then he would surely have answered her appeal for money. In any case, he would never have gone away and left his wife. His girl-friend, yes, but not a new wife.

And as Gail's mother had said, if there had never been a marriage, then Kane Farrell could refuse to take his child. Well, refuse he might, but he would never prevent Gail from leaving her behind when she herself left Vernay Downs. Left ... Suddenly aware that she had not given much thought to the return journey, she wondered just how often the Overlanding bus crossed this vast expanse of bushland. Not often, she thought, but then she dismissed the matter from her mind, deciding it was time to worry about it later. She supposed it would be possible to stay somewhere for a day or two if need be.

Dave was talking, and slanting glances at her as he did so. Having known admiration many times before, Gail was now on the alert, it being clear that Dave was attracted to her. Should she tell him that she would be leaving Vernay Downs almost as soon as she arrived? No, impossible! He would wonder what on earth was going on – and in any case, she would have to pretend that Leta was also leaving.

What a mess! What with having to bribe Leta to hold her tongue, and she herself having to be so guarded, Gail was beginning to regret her impulsiveness in requesting this lift. She felt sure that the station official, if pushed hard enough, would somehow have managed to get a car for her. He could have telephoned the nearest town for one. But even the wait for the Overlander would have been preferable to this anxiety. And the position was made even more difficult by the fact of Dave's being an employee of Leta's father. 'Why didn't I think?' she asked herself angrily. 'True, the wait at the station would have been irksome, but in the long run it would have been far less wearing on the nerves.' She turned automatically as she said this. Leta was right in the corner, her lids drooping. But she was able to make a face at Gail before she closed her eyes, allowing sleep to claim her.

'I'm glad I've had your company, Gail,' Dave was saying in his pleasant Australian drawl. 'It was bad enough being on my own coming over, but to have returned on my own – well, I'd have been bored sick without a doubt!'

'The people whom you were supposed to pick up – will you have to go back later to fetch them?'

'I don't really know.' He frowned, obviously perplexed as to why they had not arrived. 'I can't think what happened. They ought to have let the Boss know – they could have got in touch with him over the air. He'll do his block when he knows all this time's been wasted.'

'They were friends of his?'

'No, they were two men who wanted jobs. They'd worked at Vernay Downs before, as rouseabouts – that's a sort of odd-job man – but they decided they wanted to taste the delights of town life and buzzed off to Brisbane to find work. However, they've obviously had enough, because they wrote to the Boss asking for their jobs back. They were good workers, so he readily agreed to re-start them.' Dave shook his head and repeated that the Boss would be furious when he knew what had occurred. 'However,' he added with a side-long glance at her, 'he'll be glad that I found you and gave you a lift.'

'Yes.' She said no more, but felt profoundly conscious of his curiosity. She wished she could confide in him, because he was so friendly and charming towards her. 'The two men might have missed the train,' she suggested, veering the subject on to safer lines.

'They could have,' he agreed, but the frown remained. 'That won't make any difference to the Boss.'

He paused a moment. 'You haven't said much about yourself and I haven't asked because I always make a point of waiting for people to confide. If they don't talk then I conclude that it's because they don't want to. Besides, Kane Farrell's my employer and I wouldn't think of prying into his affairs. But I would like to ask how long you expect to be at Vernay Downs?'

'Not very long at all,' she replied gently. She had been going to add his name, for he had told her to call him Dave, asking at the same time if he could use her Christian name. But, somehow, she felt as if the use of his name would sound far too familiar — just this particular moment, that was.

'I see.' He glanced curiously at her. 'It's a long way to come, just for a short stay.' The element of disappointment in his voice was plain and Gail knew instinctively that he was a lonely man. 'I wish you were staying longer, Gail. I'd like to have got to know you better.'

'It isn't possible. When I've done what I came for, with Mr. Farrell, then I must go home. I live with my parents, and I have a job.'

'I see,' he said again, and lapsed into silence. Gail herself experienced a shade of disappointment that he and she would never get to know one another, and she wondered greatly at her feelings. No man had appealed to her up till now, not seriously, that was. And of course Dave did not appeal in any serious way, not at present . . . but she did wonder if, given the opportunity, she and he could have become firm friends, at least. Well, it wasn't to be, and all she was concerned with was handing over Leta to her father and then getting herself away from Vernay Downs as quickly as possible.

The long journey continued, with Leta alternately

waking – and making a nuisance of herself – and sleeping, which afforded Gail and Dave an opportunity of chatting together without the continual interruptions which invariably took the form of complaints, and which quite clearly exasperated Dave. Yet on the stops he did try to pacify the child; he had a way with him, and there were the odd times when Leta listened attentively to him, answering his questions intelligently and conversationally. He declared that she was the brightest child he had ever known, and this seemed immediately to endear him to her. He refrained from saying anything which would anger her, and once, when they had finished the snack they had been having, he asked Leta to wipe the cups when he had washed them. To Gail's utter amazement the child did as she was requested, and it certainly was a strange sight to see Leta with a tea towel in her hand, drying a cup – awkwardly, it was true, but showing willing all the same. Also, he suggested she use her toothbrush. this after an earlier display of tantrums when Gail had tried to persuade her to clean her teeth.

'I have no water,' said Leta, but Dave was already filling a cup from a flask. 'Oh, thanks,' returned Leta cheerfully on being handed this. 'I don't like cleaning my teeth, but I'll do it this once – for you!'

Gail dared not glance at him, for she knew the child so well that any sign of triumph on her part, or conveyance of congratulations to Dave, would instantly bring out the worst in the child.

'She could be trained,' was Dave's assertion later when Leta had fallen asleep. 'If I had her I'd make a nice kid out of her.' Very different this attitude from that which he had exhibited at first, thought Gail, and wondered if, when Leta was installed in the Farrell household, Dave would take over and bring about this transformation he had mentioned. Gail rather hoped he would, because she was basically sorry for Leta, even though she could not bring herself to like her. Dave lived in at the homestead, he had told her. Two other men also lived in, because they were unmarried and only those with wives were allowed to occupy the bungalows.

However, this interlude of being good was soon to be offset by Leta's getting into a temper over the length of the journey. She was fed up, she said, and wanted to go back home.

'You can't, little girl,' began Dave soothingly, when he was interrupted.

'Don't keep calling me little girl! It sounds stupid! Turn round and let's go back. I don't want to go to my—' She did break off there, and Gail uttered a great sigh which she felt sure Dave must have heard. 'I don't like sitting in a car all this time!'

'We've not very far to go now. Suppose we stop for a nice little something to eat?'

Leta said yes, they would stop, but this time when Dave asked her to clean her teeth she flatly refused, stamping her foot to give emphasis to her words.

'Come on,' he said, holding out the glass of water, but Leta did no more than knock it up, sending the water into his face. His temper flared and, seizing her by the arm, he shook her thoroughly, making no apology at all to Gail. Leta, managing to free herself, kicked him and ran away.

'I'm so sorry,' said Gail, angry and ashamed. 'I don't know what to say,' she added helplessly.

Dave's eyes met hers.

'She's not your child and yet you bring her here. But I expect you know what you're doing,' he added, watching Gail's colour heighten as embarrassment swept over her. Once again she told herself she ought not to have accepted this lift from him. But it was done now, and fortunately Dave, with his great respect for his employer, was not asking too many questions. In fact, from then on he made no further reference either to Leta or to the visit to Vernay Downs, but his silence seemed to be in itself a censure and for the rest of the journey Gail felt most uncomfortable.

It was late afternoon by the time the homestead came into view. For the past hour Leta had been at her most unpleasant, with complaint after complaint coming from the back of the car. There was a short period of peace when Leta became intensely interested in a mob of kangaroos which came into sight. They drew closer, and several emus were also to be seen. When one kangaroo came into the road she urged Dave to increase his speed so that he could hit it.

'You want the car to be wrecked?' His voice was curt and wrathful. 'What sort of a child is she?' he demanded of Gail, who mentally agreed with his following assertion that Leta would benefit from a good hiding, but of course she did not say so. Pacify the child at all costs, was her one thought, because Leta in this mood was liable to forget her promise and deliberately begin talking about her father, the man to whom she was going – Kane Farrell, Boss of Vernay Downs Station.

'Is that the house?' Leta wanted to know as they turned into the path leading to the stately homestead which, Gail suddenly recalled, Sandra had once described to her, the description having obviously been given to her by Kane Farrell.

'Yes, that's where we're going,' from Dave curtly as he slowed the car down in preparation for stopping altogether.

'I don't like it—!'

'You haven't seen it yet,' put in Gail hastily. 'You'll like it when you get there.'

Turning his head, Dave asked the question which Gail expected he would ask, and she could have slapped Leta for opening her mouth.

'Is it so important that she likes it?' Inordinately curious the tone, perplexed the stare. 'If you're not staying then what does it matter whether she likes the place or not?'

'Please, Dave, don't ask me any questions,' said Gail impulsively. 'You'll know it all soon enough – and I'm going to feel dreadful!'

The car ground slowly to a halt; turning right round in his seat, he stared at her in silence for a long moment, taking in the honest eyes, the full generous mouth, quivering slightly for she felt scared of being questioned. At length he shrugged his shoulders and said without much expression,

'You've no need to feel bad about anything, Gail. It's your own affair and therefore it has nothing to do with anyone else.'

CHAPTER THREE

ALL around the homestead, and the adjacent buildings among which were a number of bungalows, a shop and a school, lay mile upon mile of spinifex plains where numerous cattle roamed, the stockriders in their midst. Gail stood for a moment after alighting from the car, and she wondered how these men could choose so lonely a life.

'I'll see where the Boss is,' Dave was saying, a sort of impersonal formality in his voice now. 'I'll find him and tell him you're here.'

'Oh ...' She frowned in thought, experiencing a strange weakness at the knees now that the actual moment had almost arrived. 'Yes – er – tell him Miss Stafford is here.' Miss Stafford. He would remember the name, surely, and would naturally conclude that it was Sandra who was here. What would he think? Gail dismissed the question at once, since she would soon know what he was thinking!

The opening of the front door cut her musings and she turned around, as did Dave; she noticed his frown and the tightening of his mouth. A woman stood there, tall and dark, her angular figure giving the impression of arrogance, her inquiring gaze the impression of officiousness.

'What ...?' She looked from Gail to Dave, and then to the small child who was already snapping the heads from some flowers in the border. 'I saw through the window that you'd brought these two—' She broke off and told Leta to leave the flowers alone.

'I won't!'

'Leta,' sighed Gail, by now practically exhausted by

43

the child, 'come here, please.'

All Leta did was to wander farther away, towards a seat under a tree, where she sat down and swung her legs, her eyes on the woman on the step.

'Dave,' demanded Mrs. Farrell haughtily, 'what is all this? Who are these people, and where are the two rouseabouts you should have fetched?' Her dark eyes roved over him as she spoke; he made an impatient gesture, and his frown changed to a scowl. It was more than a little clear that he intensely disliked his employer's stepmother. Nevertheless, he explained as briefly as he could, bypassing the several interruptions which the woman so rudely made.

'I'll just take a walk over to the saddling paddock,' he then said hastily, before Mrs. Farrell could ask any further questions. 'The Boss might just be there. If not,' he went on looking at Gail, 'then he's with the men, and I'll have to saddle a horse and ride out to him.'

Looking in the direction indicated, Gail hoped that Kane Farrell was not too far away; she wanted to get this thing over and done with as soon as possible. Moreover, she had no desire to be left too long with Mrs. Farrell, who even now was glaring again at Leta, preparing to call over to her to stop kicking the gravel about, the multi-coloured gravel that lay on the path which Leta was now traversing, her doll, wearing only a coat, trailing along at her side, its hand in hers.

'He's over there,' Dave was saying. 'I've just caught a glimpse of him. He's the one by the bore-trough—' He pointed and, following the direction indicated, Gail saw for the first time the man whom she hated, the despicable cad who had in her opinion caused Sandra's death. He was not too far away and she could see that he was a tall man, that he sat the horse as if he were far more comfortable there than in the most luxuriously upholstered armchair. From Kane Farrell Gail

44

brought her attention to the woman standing on the step, a woman ready to ply her with questions. And, making a quick decision, she decided to take Leta over to her father at once.

Dave stared when she announced her intention of going to him, but merely shrugged when he saw her begin to walk away, calling to Leta to come to her. The child obeyed, already having been well briefed both on the plane and since. She knew she was soon to meet her father and, judging by the way she ran to Gail, she was most certainly looking forward to the encounter. Strange, unfathomable child, mused Gail as she walked briskly towards the narrow, dust-covered path on either side of which grew tussocks of myrtle-green spinifex grass, contrasting with the dainty golden wattles which abounded beneath the casuarina trees lining the banks of the creek. There never was any knowing what went on behind that preoccupied expression which Leta invariably wore.

'You're walking too quick for me,' complained Leta.

'I'm in a hurry.' Gail was afraid that the woman, unable to contain her curiosity, would come after her. But as it happened it was Dave who caught her up, by which time her heart had begun to beat abnormally and a dryness was affecting her throat. At home in England – and even on the flight and the car journey over the vast bushlands – her task had seemed simple and straightforward. But now that the time for carrying it out had arrived she felt both nervous and apprehensive. However, the vision of Sandra forced her on and her resolve never wavered.

'I'm going to speak with the Boss,' said Dave, 'so I'll walk with you.'

'I thought you said you were intending to ride?'

'I hadn't expected him to be at the bore-trough. That's no real distance.' That he wanted to be with her

45

was plain, but Gail frowned inwardly, picturing herself carrying out her task with Dave as a witness. It was unthinkable, and she said involuntarily,

'If you're wanting to see him about the two men you should have picked up, then I'll give him the message if you like?'

Dave shook his head, saying the Boss would expect the explanation to come from him and not relayed secondhand, as it were.

'You don't mind if I walk with you?' he added when involuntarily she slackened her pace.

'No, of course not.' Her mind became blocked inexplicably; she was vexed because no real picture of the scene shortly to be enacted could be focused. She was troubled about Leta, doubtful as to whether she would carry out the instructions given to her. The prospect of dolls' clothes should help, and Gail had also promised her an extra box of chocolates, which she had thoughtfully brought with her as an added bribe to the four glossy picture books and imitation gold bangle which Leta had demanded.

The distance was almost covered before Dave spoke again. He was smiling slightly as he said,

'You have the men puzzled; they're all looking this way.'

Gail saw the men staring in disbelief and supposed it was a strange sight for a woman and a little girl to be striding over this wild and ruthless terrain. It was traditionally man's country, this austere bushland called the Outback where wealthy graziers ruled like kings over their vast domains. Kane Farrell's head was also turned; a frown of puzzlement knit his brow as his lazy glance shifted from Dave to Gail before finally settling on the child. She looked as bright as a button in her coloured clothes, her gay cap and scarf. The doll still trailed at her side, forlorn and minus a shoe. Kane

Farrell, eyes narrowed against the setting sun, brought his interrogating gaze back to Dave. Gail stopped, her hand clasping that of Leta. The time seemed all wrong, she ought not to have acted precipitately. But it was done now, and anyway, Kane Farrell deserved to be shown up before his men. And so, sending him a direct look and at the same time urging Leta forward with a hand in the small of the child's back, Gail said in clear and ringing tones,

'Mr. Farrell, let me introduce your daughter! Leta, say hello to your father—'

'My—!' His expression changed to one of stupefaction and Gail was gratified to note that he was bereft of speech. She noted also the astounded expressions of the stockmen, heard the staggering exclamation that came from Dave. 'What did you say?' Slow the drawl and crisp. 'I have a feeling that I didn't hear aright?' Sliding from his horse as he spoke, Kane Farrell slowly crossed the space separating him from Gail and Leta. Gail had time to see six feet odd of perfectly formed muscle and bone before he was above her, and she tilted her head right back to look into eyes the colour of slate-grey, hard inscrutable eyes that seemed to be boring into her very mind.

'You heard aright, Mr. Farrell.' Her voice was still steady, but her heartbeats were not. Also, she was aware of a vague uneasiness because this man's manner and appearance were so very different from what she had expected. His eyes, though cold and hard, held an honest expression; his mouth was fuller and more generous than she had imagined, although there was a certain ruthlessness about it, and a firmness that spelt inflexibility. His whole bearing, though arrogant and confident, was impressive in that it gave a picture of integrity and lofty ideals. He was a man sure of himself, a man with the ability to command. He was a person

47

whom anyone, even at first glance, would not hesitate to pronounce as a man to be trusted, a man upright and conscientious. Most certainly he would never be stamped as a man who had shirked his responsibilities, who had carelessly tossed aside his moral obligations. Yet all this would appear to be contradictory, Gail reminded herself, since he *was* the father of Leta, the child he had abandoned, a child whom he knew existed but did not care *how* she existed – or how her mother existed either. And he so wealthy a man. Why, no matter how much he had sent to Sandra he would never have missed it!

Turning to Leta, Gail once again told her to say hello to her father, but before she could do so she – like Gail – heard the amused titters coming from the stockmen, some of whom had actually dismounted and drawn nearer so as not to miss anything of this free entertainment. Leta turned and glared and Gail's heart missed a beat. Leta hated to be laughed at; it riled her and she would always reveal the worst side of her nature should this happen. Gail – and indeed everyone who knew her – guarded against annoying the child in this way. But these men, totally unconscious of what they were doing, continued to titter, and in fact one man, noting that Leta's cheeks were turning bright red, as well as swelling up, started to laugh in earnest.

'You're laughing at me!' she seethed. 'Yes, you are! I hate you!' and before he could make a guess at her intention she had taken a brooch from her scarf and thrust the pin into his leg.

'Hell!' he exclaimed. 'You little brat!'

'I'll do it again – and again!' And she did, until, amid the laughter of his fellows, the man escaped by running away. Like a little wildcat Leta turned on another and gave him similar treatment.

48

'I'm afraid,' said Gail, looking up at Kane Farrell, 'that your daughter is not very well behaved. In fact—' She was interrupted by a lift of Kane Farrell's hand, but whatever he was about to say was silenced by Leta, who shouted,

'That's right, I'm not well behaved! I'm the worst little girl in the whole world! I hate people, you see, and so I like making them angry! I'd like to kill all these men for laughing at me!' She would have continued, but Kane Farrell was speaking, ordering the men to remove themselves. This they did, galloping away over the plain. Dave, uncertain and obviously just about as uncomfortable as he could be, explained about the rouseabouts, but Kane interrupted to inform him that he had received a message over the air. One man had met with an accident and was in hospital; the other would not come without him.

'I wondered if you would hear from them,' Dave said. 'I had the empty car, and this young lady wanted to come here, so—'

'That's all right – very sensible.' Kane Farrell's face was impassive, his tone completely untroubled. Dave, noting this, seemed to breathe a sigh of relief – but at the same time was amazed that his boss was remaining so calm in this present situation. 'Please leave us, Dave.'

'Yes, Boss,' and without a glance either for Gail or Leta, Dave strode briskly away towards the path along which he had come.

'And now,' drawled Kane Farrell evenly, 'perhaps you will explain?' His face was an impenetrable mask, but Gail had the impression that his mind was working at top speed.

'Your daughter,' began Gail, when she was interrupted, this time by Leta herself. The child had drawn so close to her and Kane Farrell that she was at his feet.

And like a miracle her whole manner underwent a change. Her mouth curved in a smile, her face was bright – animated, almost – and her beautiful eyes shone up at her father. Gail stared, open-mouthed, absorbing the fact that the child very much liked what she saw.

'Hello, Daddy!' she exclaimed. 'I've come to live with you because I can't live with Mummy any more. She's gone to heaven and . . .' The bright excited voice trailed away as Leta turned to Gail, a question in her eyes, her forehead wrinkled as if she were struggling mentally. 'What else did you tell me to say? I can't remember – but I'm still having my books and chocolates and dolls' clothes, remember!' A threatening finger was wagged at Gail and Kane Farrell's eyes narrowed ominously. However, it was not anger Gail detected in his expression . . . no, it was something very strange indeed. He seemed to be deep in thought, as if a plan of action had formulated in his brain. 'If you don't give me all the things you promised I'll kick and scream and pull your hair out!' Leta was continuing in a loud voice. 'It isn't my fault that I've forgotten some of the things you said I must say to my daddy!'

Gail had naturally coloured vividly at this. Kane Farrell's eyes were for a second tinged with amusement, but that something else still remained. How cool he was! It amazed Gail that, confronted like this with the child he had deserted, he could remain so unruffled. It was almost as if this sort of thing was an everyday occurrence with him, she thought, having an inexplicable desire to laugh – hysterically.

'I d-did mention that her name was Leta?' she stammered, and only then did she remember that he knew his daughter's name anyway, from the letters Sandra had sent him. 'Sandra, when she wrote to you all that time ago, would have told you everything about her

. . .' She stopped, realizing she was speaking just for the sake of it, to relieve the tension that had taken possession of her. Her voice had a cracked quality about it which seemed to be affording her listener some amusement. Yet when he spoke it was absently, and his eyes seemed to be staring into the past.

'All that time ago . . .' he was murmuring at last, repeating some of Gail's words and allowing his eyes to wander down to the child who, still at his feet, was staring up at him with a smile on her lips. He continued to stare at her with an intentness that revealed nothing to Gail. 'Yes, all that time ago.'

'Oh,' intervened Leta brightly, 'I've just remembered some more that you told me to say to my daddy—'

'Never mind,' broke in Gail, glaring at her. 'You can now be quiet while I talk to your daddy.'

But another silence followed, with Kane Farrell's face a study – unfathomable yet disturbing. His mind was on Leta, no doubt of that. What was he thinking about her behaviour? Strangely, he seemed not to be too perturbed by it, observed Gail, once again feeling that he had in mind some plan, a plan of which Leta was a part. He transferred his attention to Gail, saying quietly,

'I'm waiting for your explanation, Miss . . .?' A brow was raised inquiringly as he waited for her to answer his unspoken question.

'Stafford,' she replied briefly, and noticed his slight start of surprise.

'The same name as Sandra. Some relation?'

'Cousin.' She paused a moment, aware of the fact that she had fully expected him to deny that he was the father of Leta. 'You're obviously intending to admit that this little girl is yours?' she added, speaking her thoughts aloud.

Kane Farrell's sudden smile was ironic. He deliberately allowed her question to go by unanswered.

'Please say what you have to say, Miss Stafford.' His horse was a little distance away, cropping grass, and Leta was now interestedly watching it.

Gail explained as briefly as possible, making no effort to keep the contempt from her voice. This could not escape him and several times his eyes glinted with anger. He appeared dangerous and Gail had to give herself an impatient shake on finding herself affected by an access of trepidation.

'So her mother died three weeks ago?' Kane Farrell's eyes hardened to points of steel. Gail stared, bewildered by his manner. Yet he was apparently puzzled about something, for he shook his head from side to side, for the moment seeming to have forgotten her presence altogether. 'And she made you promise to bring this child to her father?'

'Yes, that's what I've said. She left sufficient money for the journey – it was a legacy she received from our aunt. But even had she not left money I would have brought Leta to you.' She paused a second, but he made no attempt to speak and she continued, 'She's had a dreadful time, Mr. Farrell, trying to bring up this little girl. It wasn't only the keeping of her, but the managing of her. Poor Sandra was utterly worn out—'

'There you go again!' cut in Leta, red in the face with anger. 'Everybody says I'm naughty and wicked!'

'Which of course is correct,' commented Kane Farrell mildly. 'You must learn to control your temper, my child.'

Leta put out her tongue, but then she smiled at him, and her whole expression changed. She looked positively attractive, and even cuddlesome.

'You'll have to be very firm with her,' Gail was recommending. 'Perhaps a man can do something with her—' She spread her hands in a little helpless gesture. 'I don't know – I really do not know!' A tinge of despair edged her voice and he turned to her with interest. She flushed, much to her annoyance. But this man from the Outback, this bronzed and toughened cattleman whose very appearance spoke of the great outdoors, overwhelmed her with his dominant personality, his lofty confidence, his air of superiority. She resented this attitude of his and in consequence allowed her contempt to be revealed in her expression. It was defensive, but his eyes glinted and she saw his fist close, slowly and menacingly. A quiver of awe passed through her and she wished she had seen the end of this interview and was safely aboard the Overlander and on her way home.

'Her mother could have done something, surely?' he said frowningly.

'She tried, but Leta became unmanageable. It might be of interest to you, Mr. Farrell, to know that, in the end, my cousin lost the will to live.'

His frown deepened.

'How old was she?' he inquired, and it did seem that a look of pain fleetingly crossed the tough but handsome face.

'How old?' Gail stared at him scathingly. 'You should know! She must have told you how old she was! When she died she was not quite twenty-three!'

His dark brows contracted.

'Be careful,' he warned in a cold and measured tone. 'People don't usually speak to me in that manner.'

She lowered her head, annoyed with herself that she should be intimidated by so quiet a voice. But Kane Farrell was so disconcerting, his very lack of emotion set her off balance. She had expected an angry outburst, and an attempted denial that the child was his. Instead she had met this air of calm, adopted without the slightest effort after that first astounded exclamation on suddenly being brought face to face with his daughter.

Gail spoke, unable to bear the silence any longer.

'If there are any more questions you wish to ask, Mr. Farrell,' she said in stiff and formal tones, 'then please do so. If not, perhaps you will tell me how I'm to get back to the railway station?'

Did his mouth curve slightly? His expression was strange, but certainly not amused. Nevertheless, Gail did suspect that his lips had twitched and that, inwardly, he had found something at which to smile.

'I have many questions to ask,' he told her calmly. 'But I feel they will all be answered if you relate the story to me right from the beginning.'

'The beginning?' she frowned. 'I don't know what you mean.'

He moved, turning his head in the direction of the low hills which spread away in the far distance. The sun was lowering quickly and its slanting rays threw shadows as they pierced the thin layer of cloud which had gathered suddenly. Kane Farrell's face, shaded by the broad brim of his hat, was no longer visible to Gail. She knew for sure that this hiding of it from her was deliberate. Why should he not wish her to see his expression?

'My – er – association with Sandra Stafford. You weren't there at the time—'

'I was abroad, working,' she interrupted. 'You know very well I wasn't there at the time, for if I had been you and I would have recognized one another.' She felt a prickling sensation in the region of her spine, a sensation that warned ... or was it telling her that something was not quite right about this situation? Gail decided it was a little of both.

'Yes,' he murmured almost to himself, 'we would have recognized one another.' A pause; he kept his face away from her. 'Did Sandra say we were married?'

'She did, yes.'

'I have the impression that you didn't believe her?'

'None of us believed her.'

'None of you?' He half-turned and she saw him in profile.

'My parents, and Sandra's friend – a girl who helped her a great deal, both financially and in any other way she could.'

He seemed to give a small regretful sigh, but she could not be sure about this. However, it caused her to speak impulsively, asking if he were feeling some degree of remorse. At this he turned sharply, dark anger in his gaze. But whatever he had been going to say was bitten back and instead she heard the one brief word,

'Perhaps.'

Her mouth curved with contempt.

'A little late, don't you think?' with undisguised sarcasm. 'Had you known qualms sooner then Sandra wouldn't be where she is now.' Strong words, and she was not at all surprised to see the angry colour creep along the sides of his jaw. However, once again he held his tongue ... and once again Gail experienced that feeling that he was planning something. She thrust it away, mainly because she could not be sure the impression was not born of her imagination. She asked outright if he had married her cousin. No answer was forthcoming; instead, Kane Farrell put a few more questions to her, questions which she answered, but at the same time reminding him that he already knew the answers.

'You were there! You're the one involved, so I fail to see why you should want me to tell you about Sandra, and the date when Leta was born and all the rest. She wrote telling you about Leta, and I expect she asked you to send her money?'

Was it imagination, she wondered, or had his eyes suddenly taken on an expression of regret?

'Yes, she did ask me for money,' he said, almost inaudibly. And he added, in no more than a whisper now, 'I should have sent her some . . . yes, I should—' He stopped, aware that he had a listener. Gail saw at once that he had been speaking to himself. She said involuntarily,

'I can't believe – somehow – that you're such a cad as I first branded you.'

His swift smile was sardonic.

'I'm flattered,' he said crisply, and then he added, 'You're outspoken if nothing else, Miss Stafford.'

'Naturally we've all branded you a cad!'

He glanced to where Leta was sitting, on a fallen tree trunk which was lying not far from where his horse was cropping the grass.

'In every situation,' he said slowly, 'there are parts unknown.' He looked seriously at her. 'I make a point of never condemning unless I have proof that condemnation is deserved. I want to ask you, Miss Stafford, to remember this.'

She lowered her lashes, acutely conscious of a rebuke.

'You've shirked your duty; you'll own to that?'

He allowed that to pass and said,

'You asked just now if I was married to your cousin. You obviously sorted out her papers after she had died?'

Gail's eyes widened. It was just as if he were pumping her – subtly asking if she had found a marriage certificate! If he *were* married to Sandra, then there most certainly would have been a marriage certificate in existence. He must know this. Puzzled in the extreme, and acutely conscious of that tingling sensation which seemed to warn that something was not quite right, she asked herself why Kane Farrell was so cautiously avoiding a direct answer. He knew whether or not he had been married to Leta's mother. Of course he knew . . . and yet he appeared to be probing to discover whether or not any proof of a marriage existed. Gail shook her head bewilderedly, and stared at him with a questioning gaze.

'I didn't find a marriage certificate,' she said, and then, 'Mr. Farrell, were you married to Sandra?' Surely he could not continue to avoid answering her, thought Gail, and she was right. He was hesitating, but she saw by his expression that an answer would this time be forthcoming.

'No . . . I was not married to Leta's mother.'

Silence except for the sudden whinnying of the horse and the following exclamation with which Leta responded to it. Gail was still staring up into Kane Farrell's dark countenance, her mind going over what he had just said. There had been the hesitation, and the rather odd inflection in his tone, and it was his tone rather than the words themselves which puzzled her. Also puzzling to her was her own state of mind, for one moment she was condemning him while the next she was telling herself that he could not be so heartless as it appeared on the surface.

'Parts unknown . . .' So grave the voice, and a warning in the slate-grey eyes. What did he mean? Had there been some excuse for his conduct? But no. Gail would not have it. He had received Sandra's letter; he had admitted this, and he had also admitted that he should have sent her money.

'You're a strange man,' she sighed, not to him, but merely murmuring her thoughts aloud. 'I wish I understood.'

No response from Kane Farrell; his brow was furrowed and even yet again she had the impression that he had some plan in mind.

'Tell me,' he said at length, 'why was there no one who would take the child?'

'Because I'm so naughty!' from Leta who had risen and come towards him. 'I'm bad, very bad! Mrs. Renshawe down our lane said I was the devil's she-cub —' She broke off, frowning. 'What's a cub? I thought it was a little baby lion.' She looked up at him. 'If it is then I'm not a cub, am I?' she added, diverted to such an extent that the expression in her eyes was one of wonderment — rather an attractive expression, thought Gail, recalling how at times her expression could be so vicious that she looked almost ugly.

'No,' he said unsmilingly, 'you're not a cub.' Still thoughtful, Gail noticed, and she wished she could see what was going on in his mind.

'Oh, a beetle!' Leta bent down; the brooch was still in her hand and she was all ready to stick the pin in the insect when Gail snatched at her wrist and dragged her away.

'You naughty girl! How many times have I told you that it hurts little creatures when you treat them like that!' She was furious, and for the moment Kane Farrell was completely forgotten.

'I like hurting them! I'll stick it in you in a minute! And I'll stick it ten times in that lady, because I don't like her! You know, the lady we saw at Daddy's house!'

'Lady?' Kane looked at Gail, the words of censure he had been going to say to Leta having been stemmed for the present. 'She had black hair?'

'That's right.'

Kane's eyes took on a darkling expression, but at the same time he had that faraway look mingling with it. Gail waited, half expecting him to make some further reference to the woman who was his stepmother. But he lapsed into a silence and she began to stir restlessly. At length she asked about the Overlander, adding that she wished to get away from here as soon as possible.

Turning lazily, he regarded her with a mild inscrutable stare before he said, staggering her so that she could only gape at him unbelievingly,

'If my daughter stays then you stay too, Miss Stafford.'

'W-what did you say?' she managed at last.

'I believe you heard me.' Totally unaffected by this moment which was to Gail overcharged, he took up the reins which he had previously hooked over the broken branch of a eucalpyt. 'You don't leave Leta with me unless you stay with her.'

'Don't be ridiculous!' Her mind was so confused that she scarcely knew what she was saying. But she was acutely aware of the impregnable, granite-like quality of his face, and also of the fact that, should he prove to be immovable, then the whole point and purpose of her journey here would be destroyed. 'It's quite impossible for me to stay!' She gestured with her hands, her mind still clouded by what he had said. 'This ultimatum's stupid! What would I want to stay in a place like this for?'

Ignoring this, he said calmly,

'I need a mother for my child.'

'You must be out of your mind!'

'On the contrary,' he rejoined smoothly, 'my mind was never more ordered.'

'But—'

'I have no intention of entering into any argument,'

he broke in gently. 'It should be plain to you that I can't have Leta unless I also have someone to look after her.'

'You want a nanny? But you said a *mother*.'

'A mother, yes.'

Gail made another impatient gesture with her hands.

'What are you trying to say, Mr. Farrell?'

His grey eyes seemed to smile with amusement.

'I'm not offering you marriage,' he began, then stopped a second or two to watch the colour creep into her cheeks. 'All the same, it's a mother I want for Leta – not a nanny.' He paused a moment as Leta came closer to him. She looked up and smiled. He flicked a finger and to Gail's utter amazement the child instantly obeyed the unspoken command and moved away, out of earshot. 'What I want is for you to pose as my wife— No, please don't interrupt me! I want you to pose as my long-lost wife. We parted – a misunderstanding or silly quarrel caused it – but now we've come together again, a happy family—'

'You *are* out of your mind,' she interrupted, but even as the words left her lips the truth burst in upon her. So there *had* been some basis for her suspicions that he was planning something!

'Either you remain here with Leta or you take her back to England with you,' Kane Farrell was saying implacably. 'And if you do take her back, then you mustn't trouble me with her ever again.' He sounded callous, she thought, but she made no comment, her mind being totally absorbed by what she had discovered. Kane Farrell wanted her, Gail, to pose as his wife, so taking his stepmother's place as mistress of his home. And of course Leta was an important part of the plan; a few weeks of that little delinquent and Mrs. Farrell would know only one way to turn – towards the door!

It was an ingenious scheme, and it had come to Kane when he saw what kind of a child his young daughter was. She would quite literally drive his step-mother out, he had concluded. Gail had to smile despite the tenseness of the scene. How fortunate Kane must have felt himself to be – with his daughter coming along at a time like this!

'Mr. Farrell—' she began, when he interrupted her to say,

'Kane's the name. I'm sure I've made myself clear,' he went on to add. 'Either you both stay here, at Vernay Downs, or you both leave. The choice is yours.'

'I've already made my choice. It's impossible for me to stay, even if I wanted to, which I don't. I have a job; I live with my parents – I'm their only child— Oh, the whole proposition's so absurd that it's not worth my entering into explanations as to why I can't accept it!' She spoke resolutely, meaning every word she uttered, so why this subconscious thrusting away of the intruding vision of life out here, in this wild and lonely land with its endless plains, its strange animals and trees, its perverse climate and the almost feudal manner in which most of its properties were run.

'In that case, there's no more to be said. I'll arrange for you and Leta to be taken back to the station—' He broke off and turned, as did Gail. Leta, obviously having heard what was being said, was standing just behind Kane Farrell . . . and her lovely eyes were brimming with tears.

'Aren't I staying with my daddy, after all?' she cried, stepping towards Gail and clutching her skirt with both hands, having dropped her doll on to the ground. 'Why won't you stay, Gail? I want to have a daddy of my own . . .' The tears flowed, but before Gail could stoop to comfort her she ran away and sat down on the

61

fallen tree trunk, then began rocking herself to and fro, crying softly, 'I wanted a daddy, like Susan and Diana and Emma. I wanted a daddy of my own . . .'

Gail looked up at Kane Farrell, and his eyes flickered strangely as he noted the tears in hers.

'I had no idea she could be like this,' she quivered, 'What must I do—?' She stopped, astounded by her weakness . . . and yet how could she ignore the plight of Sandra's child? No use telling herself that, having honoured her promise by bringing the child here, she could not help it if all had not gone according to the wishes of her mother. No, that was shirking the issue. And if she did shirk then she would be no less blameworthy than Kane Farrell himself. And yet Leta, despite this moment of weeping for her father, was still Leta – the unbridled creature for whom no one had ever had a good word.

'I could never manage her!' Gail was distressed and it showed. Kane Farrell's expression became exceedingly curious as he watched the quiver of her lips, the rapid blinking of her eyelids as she endeavoured to prevent the tears from falling on to her cheeks. He moved, restlessly, and his brow was furrowed in a frown. She saw a movement in his throat, as if he were swallowing with difficulty something that had lodged there. 'No, I could never manage her!'

'I'll be good!' The cry came urgently, but Leta remained motionless on the trunk of the tree. 'Stay, Gail! Stay here so that I can stay too! I want to have a daddy of my own!'

Although she felt dreadful about it, Gail resolutely ignored Leta's first sentence, since she knew for sure that she could not be good if she tried. And she never did try! There was in her a bit of the devil himself and nothing less than a miracle would drive it out.

'I can't stay . . .' But her voice faltered to silence. It

was not only Leta's plight that was driving her from the path of reason; it was also the man himself, Kane Farrell, Boss of Vernay Downs cattle station, who was responsible for this swinging of her emotions. It was as if he possessed some impelling mental pressure with which he could bend her to his will. Reprehensible he might be, yet she was puzzled because there seemed to be so much about him that was contradictory. She was unable to fight against the attractiveness of him, vaguely wondering if it was partly his outward appearance which affected her – his powerful physique or tough, sun-bitten good looks. Or was it solely his dynamic personality and aristocratic air?

She shook her head, her mind too clouded in any case for her to be able to find an answer to so difficult a question. He began to speak, rather gently and with what could only be described as infinite understanding. His confidences went in his favour and as he continued she found herself carried away on a tide of helplessness until, in the end, her decision was made and she gave him her answer. He smiled and thanked her; she knew a half pleasant, half disturbing tingling sensation rippling throughout her body.

Had she made her own decision, or had it been made for her by some subtle mechanism worked by Kane Farrell? More important, had she made the right decision? Gail just had to mention this to Kane, speaking impulsively and with a tremor of anxiety in her voice.

'Yes, Gail,' he said gently, 'you have made the right decision. Have no doubts about it; you'll not regret what you're doing.'

She looked up at him, and then down at Leta. The child's eyes were shining through her tears and a smile trembled on her lips.

'She looks so ... different,' murmured Gail, dazed

and wondering where the familiar mulish expression had gone.

'People do,' returned Kane in his quiet unhurried tone, 'when they're happy.'

Gail shook her head, more bewildered than ever by this strange man who obviously had two very contrasting parts to his nature.

'I don't understand how you came to neglect her for so long,' she just had to say, and in return Kane said, looking directly at her,

'Remember what I said about parts unknown?' And when she nodded her head, 'Try to keep that in mind, Gail — it might help you in the difficult task which you've taken on.'

CHAPTER FOUR

THE sun was setting and in the garden a couple of kookaburras sat on the forked branch of a white gum tree and growled throatily. Leta, walking with Gail along the path bordering the shrubbery, gave a loud laugh, then complained pettishly when the jackos failed to join in.

'Why don't they laugh?'

'They will, when they're ready.' Gail, enchanted by the marbled effect of light and shade brought about by the ever lowering angle of the sun's rays, had no ear for the murmurings of a fractious child, even though it was her job to look after her.

'Why aren't they ready now?'

'They seem to laugh more in the mornings.' Her eyes wandered to the long line of mountains, the MacDonnall Ranges, rising above the more gentle landscape, their peaks crimson on the sky line. And as she watched there appeared the dark silhouette of a brumby, a magnificent creature with mane flowing as it raced across her line of vision. Nearer to, and with considerably less movement, could be seen two Aborigine stockriders, appearing to glide about among the mob of cattle roaming the plain. Excellent horsemen and musterers, their numbers were high on Vernay Downs Station. Kane Farrell always spoke in praise of them.

'I know they laugh in the mornings! But why don't they laugh all the time?'

'Because they'd get tired. You'd get tired if you laughed all the time.' The shadows were deepening on the plains and Gail had the impression of a vast sea of darkest blue. 'Come, it's getting dark; we must go in.'

'I want the jackos to laugh first!'

'I want – I want – I want!' The interruption came from the woman sitting on the front verandah, the words being called in a raised tone so that they would be heard. Turning her head, Leta put out her tongue before twisting her face into the most grotesque lines.

'Mind your own business, Mrs. Nosey-Parker! Go in and shut your door!'

'Leta!' began Gail, then realized that the child's father was there, having approached silently after leaving his horse, Golden Light, in the tender care of Jimmy, the Abo rouseabout.

Kane Farrell's glance was stern, but to Gail's surprise he made no attempt to admonish his daughter. Instead, he put out a hand to ruffle her hair.

'Happy?' he asked her, but his eyes were on Gail's face.

'Yes, Daddy, I'm happy!'

'Do you know how long you've been here?'

'One week and one day!'

'That's right. Good girl for keeping count.'

'I'm not a good girl,' chuckled Leta, seizing his hand and putting it to her cheek. 'I'm a very naughty girl!' She glanced slyly at him. 'You don't want me to be good, do you, Daddy?'

Was he put out by this? wondered Gail, trying to read that impenetrable expression even though she knew the futility of her efforts. For what Leta said was true; her father had no desire for an immediate reformation in his errant daughter . . . no, not until his plan had succeeded. And after that? A wry expression entered Gail's eyes. Young Leta was in for a shock! Gail had never been so sure of anything as she was of Kane's ability to bring his child to heel. A week in his house had more than proved to her the supreme mastery of the man, even though she had seen little of him, as he

66

was out for practically the whole of each day, returning to the homestead merely for lunch and then at dusk, when he was finished work – at least, outside. After dinner he usually went off to a private room of his own – an office-cum-snug – one of the lubras had termed it one day when Gail had met her coming from the room, which she had just been cleaning.

'You haven't answered my question,' Leta was saying. 'You don't want me to be good, do you?'

'I've never said such a thing.' His voice to Gail held an edge that warned, but it was not meant to be heard by Leta and as she continued to look at Kane, Gail could not suppress a smile. His eyebrows shot up inquiringly.

'Something amusing you, Gail?'

She nodded, but glanced at the verandah. Following the direction of her eyes Kane nodded too, but he made no comment and Leta began chattering, demanding to know how she could make the kookaburras laugh.

'You can't. They laugh when they feel like it, just as you do.'

'If I tell them they must—'

'You can't order them the way you order people,' chided Gail. She was awkward in Kane's company, as always, and she would have escaped were it at all possible. She had no desire to be with him, and this was – she admitted quite freely – owing to the manner in which she was affected by him. She had hated him before meeting him and she intended to go on hating him, because of what he had done to Sandra. But the more she saw of him the more she was torn by doubts, not only that there might have been some excuse for his conduct, but that she herself might reach the point when she no longer even disliked him.

'Do you generally order people about?' he was inquiring of Leta and, when the child said yes, he then added, 'I think I must get to know you a little better, young lady. Eight days you've been here and I still know practically nothing about you.'

'You know her character – to a great extent,' put in Gail shortly.

'I know she's not well-behaved, yes.'

'Her mother was so gentle and unoffending,' mused Gail without thinking.

'So Leta doesn't take after her? Is that what you're telling me?'

He had asked for it, decided Gail, and she answered, looking directly up into his face,

'It is, yes.'

'So she must take after me?'

'That's what I was implying,' she returned with honesty, and to her surprise, his only reaction was to say, with a quality of amused satire in his voice,

'I won't argue with you, my dear.'

My dear . . . She wished he would not say it; it always awakened some strong but unfathomable emotion within her.

'Do you mind if I go inside?' she asked, constraint in her manner. 'I would like to wash my hair before dinner.'

'By all means,' he assented. They had drawn nearer to the verandah and were now so close that his step-mother was able to hear what they said. And for her benefit he put his arm around Gail's shoulder and touched her cheek with his lips, an action which he had done once before, and which then, as now, left her blushing adorably.

Gladly she made her escape to the elegant bedroom which had its spectacular view to the mountains whose summits were now bathed in the honey light of evening. She was glad to be alone because Leta was a drag on the nerves. No improvement had taken place, and none would until Kane Farrell's purpose was served and his stepmother and her daughter driven out of Vernay Downs.

Sitting down on a chair, Gail leant back among the cushions, determined to relax for a few minutes before washing her hair. And not unnaturally her thoughts took a backswitch, drifting on what were now familiar lines, since on the rare occasions when she was alone, she invariably went over that unforgettable scene which had culminated in her accepting Kane Farrell's offer.

He had confided in her the reason for his wanting her to pose as his wife; he had offered her a salary quite beyond her wildest dreams; he had promised that, at the end of her stay, he would give her a lump sum and also pay all the expenses incurred by her return trip to England. He would keep Leta, he had promised – although Gail sensed a strange hesitancy before he answered her question about this.

'She's your daughter,' Gail had said, 'and if I do this for you you must promise to keep her.' It was then that he had seemed to hesitate. Nevertheless, once he had made the promise, Gail had not the smallest doubt that he would honour it.

Immediately after she had accepted his offer they discussed the problem of Leta.

'She's extremely intelligent,' Gail informed him, 'so she'll grasp what you want to tell her. She'll carry out the instructions if you bribe her—'

'Bribe?' he murmured, at this moment bending down as he made some billy tea for them to drink while the discussions were taking place, and the necessary plans made. 'Bribe?' he repeated, glancing at his daughter.

'She usually has to have chocolates and toys—' Gail was interrupted by Kane's quiet,

'Leta will do as she's told without being bribed. Am I right, child?' he added, and Leta, although pouting first — merely from force of habit — said yes, he was right. At which he threw his 'wife' a look of sardonic amusement not unmingled with triumph. 'You don't know how to handle her,' he murmured, straightening up and handing Gail a cup of tea. 'Come here,' he ordered Leta, and she came to him at once. 'Now, do you really want to stay here with me?'

'Of course. I want to have a daddy of—'

'Yes, you've already told me that. But you heard me say that you could only stay if Gail stayed too.'

'Yes — you know I heard, because I cried when she said she wouldn't stay.'

'She's staying now, as you know.'

'I'm glad she is — but I don't like her much because she doesn't like me—'

'Gail is staying so that you can stay!' he interrupted sternly. 'What do you mean, you don't like her?'

'I don't like any people — only you, and Dave.'

Her father ignored this, going on to explain, slowly and carefully, exactly what he wanted of her. 'So whether you like Gail or not you've to learn to call her Mummy. And mind you don't forget—' He wagged a warning finger at her. 'If you do, and you call her Gail, then off you go, back to England!'

The child actually went pale.

'I might forget,' she began, and for the first time ever Gail saw her troubled. 'I must try hard not to forget.'

'And the next thing,' continued Kane when he felt sure that he was making himself felt, 'is that you never answer any questions which people in the house might ask. Is that also clear?'

Leta's forehead wrinkled.

'If I do you'll send me home again?'

Smiling faintly at her way of putting it, her father

said yes, he would send her home immediately, if she disobeyed his order.

'I won't answer any questions,' she returned, brightening up all at once. 'I don't like people asking me questions anyway. I always tell them to mind their own business!'

He frowned at this and glanced at Gail.

'Is that true?'

She gave a grimace.

'Perfectly true.'

'Well, it serves our purpose for the time being.'

'I'm the rudest little girl on earth,' piped in Leta with a chuckle. 'Another lady down our street said so.'

'So it would seem,' grimly from her father. 'However, as I said, it will serve our purpose.' This to Gail, who nodded in agreement before putting the cup to her mouth and sipping the hot tea. Kane took a drink, his expression thoughtful as he mused on what other instructions he must give to Leta. There were several; she listened, her eyes alert, intelligent, and he was pleased with what he saw. 'She'll do,' he declared with satisfaction. 'She's a very bright little girl.'

'Dave said that as well!'

'Is that why you like him?'

'Yes – but I like him for other things as well. He doesn't keep saying I'm wicked like other people. And when they say I'm wicked I want to be *very* wicked!'

'Seems reasonable,' nodded her father thoughtfully. 'I think I'd feel the same.'

Gail gave a little start of surprise.

'You're encouraging her,' she almost snapped. 'When you know her better, Mr. Farrell—'

'Kane's the name, remember. You're my wife.'

She coloured vividly and looked away, Kane gave a small laugh and would have turned his attention to

71

Leta again, but Gail decided to finish what she had been saying.

'When you know her better, you'll realize that she needs no encouragement to be naughty!'

He looked at her in silence for a space, a slight frown knitting his brows.

'You're not a psychologist, are you, Gail?'

'I did once wonder if her trouble was psychological,' was the defensive response.

'Certainly it's psychological,' he pronounced emphatically. 'There's no doubt at all—'

'What does that long word mean?' interposed Leta with interest.

'Nothing you would understand,' answered Gail, before Kane could do so. 'Look, your doll's in that bush over there. You'll not find her if it gets dark.'

Leta went off and Kane said,

'That poor child's been ill-treated.'

Her eyes opened very wide.

'Ill-treated!' she gasped.

'There are more ways than one of ill-treating people. Physically she's been pampered, but mentally she's been neglected. Being of much higher than average intelligence she's alert to everything that's said about her, to the attitudes adopted towards her.' He paused and set his mouth. 'Frankly, if people kept on telling me I was wicked, then I'd do my damnedest to prove them correct!'

She stared, half expecting to see a hint of amusement on his face; all she saw was anger.

'I believe you would,' she murmured. 'Yes, I believe you would.'

After making sure that Leta understood exactly what she must and must not do, Kane took her and Gail back to the homestead where he had firmly handed his daughter over to Daisybell, one of the three house girls whose duties were to keep the house clean and see to the cooking and the laundry. He had then taken Gail to a small sitting-room where a log fire was set in the low stone hearth. The fire was unlighted but ready for a match to be put to it should this prove to be necessary. A rather shabby but comfortable couch, at an angle by the window, looked inviting, and Gail found herself moving towards it even before she was invited to sit down. It was then that Kane had finalized his plan, answering any questions which Gail put to him. She was told that messages could be sent quickly over the air, and that it would not be too long before her parents were informed of her decision to accept the post of nanny to Leta. Gail had already mentioned that she would have to tell her parents that she was staying in the capacity of nanny, saying they would consider her quite mad if they knew the truth – that she was posing as his wife.

'They're going to think it most odd,' she had to say, and in her voice Kane detected a note of deep anxiety. 'You see, they know full well that caring for Leta is the very last job I would take on.' Or the last job anyone else would take on, she added, but to herself.

'You can explain that I believe she can improve with the right treatment – and handling.'

'You do believe this?' she had asked him curiously, and without hesitation he had nodded emphatically.

'I'm sure of it,' he said. And after a small silence he went on, eyeing her curiously, 'You are not too perturbed about your parents' reaction to this rather unorthodox decision of yours – does this mean that they are the kind of parents I admire most, the kind that don't interfere?'

She smiled spontaneously, and her eyes brightened. Kane, watching her, became intent, and faintly interested. He appeared to be discovering what she

73

looked like. Out in the open the sun had been setting when first she had approached him, and in consequence the light had become duller and duller as the moments passed. Now she was under a bright light, with every line and contour of her face revealed.

'Yes, they are. I'm most fortunate in my parents. And although they'll be worried at first, which is only natural, they won't ask me to change my mind. They never have interfered — not since I was old enough to know my own mind and make my own decisions.'

'Well, that simplifies matters. Everything appears to be simple.'

'Simple?' she echoed, staring at him. 'You're far more confident than I. I foresee many difficulties ahead before, my task done, I'm able to return home.'

Faintly he smiled.

'I rather think,' he said thoughtfully, 'that Leta will be of tremendous help.'

She slanted a glance at him; it was almost an admonishment.

'Don't you think it's cheating, to do it this way?'

'No such thing. I've given my stepmother the offer of another home, a very lovely home, but she stubbornly remains here . . .' He paused and seemed more deep in thought than before. Gail wondered if he had been going to say that he knew just why his stepmother was staying — in order that her daughter might stay too, and therefore continue to have an opportunity of securing Kane as a husband. However, he refrained from mentioning the daughter and merely went into one or two more details, minor details which Gail herself had overlooked. Finally he asked her her age.

'I shall have to know it,' he added wryly, 'also your birthday.'

'I'm twenty-three, and my birthday's on the twenty-seventh of next month.'

'So soon? We shall have to have a party, you see – just for effect.'

She said nothing; she could not imagine a party being given for her. Who would come? There seemed to be no one else living in this lonely terrain of endless spinifex plains. That was, no one other than the small community of stockmen, their wives and children, all of whom lived in the attractive bungalows which Gail had seen clustered on a rise some small distance from the homestead.

'Well,' Kane was saying, 'if you've nothing more to clear up we'll go and see where my stepmother is.'

'It's going to be an ordeal,' she faltered. 'Is she going to be convinced?'

The slate grey eyes took on a sort of languid expression. He said carelessly,

'She has no alternative.'

'But she's bound to ask a whole lot of questions.'

'She can ask away; it doesn't mean she'll get them answered.' Implacable the tone, tight the mouth. Gail decided that Mrs. Farrell would be the first to retire from any battle of words which might take place.

The meeting did not prove to be so much of an ordeal as Gail expected. Blandly and without hesitation or preamble, Kane had said,

'Rachel, I want you to meet my wife, Gail; and my daughter, Leta.'

'Your—!' The woman gaped, staring in astounded silence at her stepson before transferring her dark and venomous gaze to Gail and, finally, to Leta. 'Your wife!' She stopped again and shook her head. Gail noted the colour in her face change from pink to crimson and then to a sort of sickly grey. 'What are you talking about?' She looked at Kane as if he had taken leave of his senses. 'You have no wife – no daughter !'

75

'Mother, what's going on? You're not quarrelling with Kane again? You shouldn't . . .' The voice came from the girl who had just entered the room. Soft and purring, it had come to a slow and questioning stop as the girl, tall, dark and very beautiful in an exotic kind of way, suddenly noticed Gail and Leta. 'Who are these?' She looked up at Kane, and smiled faintly at him. 'Friends of yours? But how did they get here?'

'Ertha, meet my wife,' interrupted Kane calmly in the same bland tone. 'This little one is my daughter, Leta.' Fondly he ruffled her hair; she responded by taking his hand in hers and holding tightly on to it.

'Your wife?' The dark eyes opened wide in a disbelieving stare. 'Is this some kind of a joke?' she queried, far less troubled than her mother, and Gail saw at once that she actually did believe it was a joke. Surely she knew the Boss of Vernay Downs better than that, thought Gail who, even in the short time she had been acquainted with him, had learned that he was a man who had no time for trivialities, a man serious of disposition, firm of resolve.

'Where have they come from?' demanded Mrs. Farrell without affording Kane time to reply to her daughter's query. 'Dave brought them; he told me he picked them up at the station.'

'That's correct.'

'Kane,' intervened Ertha, taking a step towards him, 'you didn't answer my question.'

'It isn't a joke, Ertha. Gail's my wife— No, please don't interrupt or we'll be here far longer than suits me. Gail and I were married when I went over to England on holiday, long before you came here. But we were estranged – some silly misunderstanding causing the rift. Recently I heard that I had a daughter and, as you can imagine, I felt I must see her. So I sent for Gail—'

'You sent for her?' Ertha looked suspiciously at him. 'You've never given us any intimation that you were expecting these two.'

'Nor was Dave expecting to pick them up,' added her mother, her voice still harsh and cracked but a little quieter than before.

'There's been a slight misunderstanding. Gail should have arrived next Tuesday, and not this Tuesday.'

Gail looked at him, her feelings mixed. She admired his handling of this situation, admitting that the lies were necessary, and yet, paradoxically, she was more than a little shocked that any man could lie with such suave self-possession. When she herself told a necessary untruth, she invariably gave herself away by colouring up.

'I still don't believe you! And I'm not having these two in the house!'

'*You* are not having them?' Dangerous the tone now, and Gail felt a shudder pass through her whole body. How very forbidding he was in this particular mood! 'As always,' he went on in tones of ice, 'you speak without thinking. Gail as my wife has a position here – an important position. She is from now on the mistress of my home!'

Silence; Gail wondered if the woman was going to have some kind of a fit, so deep was the colour of her face. Ertha, on the other hand, was standing like one frozen to the spot. It was a dramatic scene, with the air electrified, and yet Gail was strangely unaffected, and afterwards when she tried to explain this, she could only reach the conclusion that her mind was too dazed for very much to penetrate. She was immune to the glares of the woman, and to the cold malicious stare of her daughter.

'I still don't believe she's your wife!' Mrs. Farrell was plainly making some attempt to be calm, but her

fury was proving too much for her. That she was bewildered was clear; she seemed to be accepting the fact
that Gail was Kane's wife even while declaring her
disbelief. 'You say you were married while on holiday
in England? Your father never mentioned this fact to
me.'

'The fact of my being on holiday, or the fact of my
marriage?'

'Neither,' she returned, her teeth snapping
together.

'He never knew about the marriage. And as for his
mentioning the holiday — why should he mention it? I
don't expect he told you everything he and I did in the
years before he met you. After all, you were married to
him for less than a year.'

'I am not accepting this story! This child — I refuse
to believe she's yours. Why, she hasn't even the faintest
look of you—'

'I am his daughter!' flashed Leta who, much to
Gail's amazement, had up till now been most restrained, merely being an interested listener. Still cling-
ing to Kane's hand, she went on, her eyes as wicked as
Gail had ever seen them, 'He's my daddy — my own
daddy! So you shut up and mind your own business!
Gail's my mummy, and if you say again that my daddy
tells lies I'll kick you!'

'Bravo!' said Kane, but softly.

'Kane!' gasped Ertha.

'The insolent, ill-behaved creature!' Mrs. Farrell,
her bosom heaving, threw the child a virulent look.
'You are going back where you came from!' and she
made the fatal mistake of wagging a forefinger before
Leta's face. Swift as lightning the child had seized it
and put it in her mouth. Even Gail winced as she saw
the vicious little teeth do their work.

'Oh!' screamed Mrs. Farrell. 'Ertha — oh, I believe I

shall faint!' And in fact her angular figure did sway as the finger was released. Kane took a step forward, but his aid was unnecessary. Ertha was at her mother's side, and she spoke quietly as she said,

'Come, Mother, let's get out of here. We'll talk in private.' She looked at Kane. 'I don't know what to think,' she told him. 'If your story's true, then it's a very strange one indeed.'

'It's true, all right,' was his firm rejoinder. 'I hope Ertha, that you will be able to convince your mother that she is no longer mistress here.'

CHAPTER FIVE

HER reflections having come to an end, Gail rose from her chair and, going into the bathroom, washed her hair. A few minutes later she was drying it, and then she brushed it until it shone, the copper tints profoundly attractive as they caught the light. She stared for a long moment at her reflection, more happy now with what she saw, and the wide generous mouth curved in a smile. Her skin was clear and pale; she touched her cheeks with colour and smiled again. There was a strange sensation within her, a sensation she had experienced before, when she knew she was looking especially attractive.

The dress she chose was scooped low at the neck, and it was sleeveless. The skirt flared out, short and crisp. On impulse she swung around on her toes, wondering why she should feel so lighthearted when life was, in the main, rather difficult.

Firstly there was Mrs. Farrell, and her daughter. Antagonists both, as was to be expected of course. Then there was Leta, difficult as ever and with no sign of an improvement. Kane himself, kind but so cool and impersonal when they were alone, though putting on an act when the other two women were present. And, lastly, there was Dave . . .

How disappointed he had been in her. She had not known what to say to him, a truthful answer being impossible. She had spoken to Kane about it, explaining that she had told him Leta was not hers. Kane had merely expressed amusement, finally telling her that she need not worry herself about Dave; he was just an employee and would not be interested anyway. But Gail knew differently, owing to Dave having expressed the wish to know her better. However, she could scarcely tell Kane this, so she allowed the matter to drop. But she felt she would like to talk to Dave some time, and apologize for the lies she had told – which of course were not lies at all, but poor Dave believed they were.

'You look charming, my dear.' Kane's voice greeted her the moment she stepped into the elegant dining-room with its oak furniture and silver candelabra. On the sideboard large silver dishes gleamed in the light from above. A cosy atmosphere pervaded the room, which had in part retained its nineteenth-century flavour even though the homestead, like others in the Outback, boasted the modern amenities such as central heating and air-conditioning. Most of the rooms, however, still had their open hearths where log fires burned on cold evenings, their flames shedding warm and gentle lights on to heavy leather couches and broad oak beams. In the massive kitchen with its slatted roof and wooden ceiling supports stood a cast-iron stove which burned wood and on which was prepared the enormous meals with which the stockmen satisfied their hearty appetites. Daisybell, a favourite with them because of her skill as a cook, produced among other things the most delicious scones and biscuits, these for the men to take out with them, to have with their billy tea instead of the more conventional damper which they cooked themselves out there, in the open.

'Thank you, Kane.' As usual, Gail felt awkward in his presence, and at times like this it was even worse, owing to the watchful and antagonistic eyes of Mrs. Farrell and Ertha.

Kane was opening a bottle of wine, and this he put on the table. Dave entered looking spruce in light flannels and a clean blue-shirt; he wore a tie, whereas the other men, Bevis and Chuck, wore cravats tucked loosely into the open-necked shirts they wore. Kane was in a linen suit of light blue, his white shirt gleaming against his throat.

Leta was allowed to stay up for dinner on two evenings a week, and this was one of those evenings. She sat on her father's left, next to Dave. As usual, she had her various complaints, and these she was allowed to voice without interruption or censure from her father. Gail would at times protest and begin to threaten her, but invariably Kane would interfere, telling Gail that Leta was merely going through one particular stage of child development.

'Child development?' from Mrs. Farrell wrathfully. 'How can you say a thing like that?' At times when others were present she was restrained, since she had no intention of putting herself in a humiliating situation by affording her stepson an opportunity of asserting his authority. 'What do you know about children?'

'Enough to be able to say that my daughter is developing quite naturally.'

Even Gail gave a tiny gasp at this. Kane, however, was calmly filling up Dave's wineglass before paying attention to his own. But he avoided Gail's swift glance, quite deliberately, and began talking to Bevis, a tall and lanky stockman who had worked at Vernay Downs since he was a boy of sixteen, having come as a rouseabout but who was now one of the best horsemen on the station. Bronzed of face and tough, he had a serious disposition – something like Kane's, Gail had already decided – and would often be found, sitting on the front verandah after dinner, deep in thought.

Chuck was sturdier in appearance, with muscles like knotted rope. He too was tanned and toughened by the outdoor life. A bachelor like Dave and Bevis, he had made Vernay Downs his permanent home, and was treated by Kane as one of the family. Not by Mrs. Farrell, however, who made no pretence of the fact that she would have made all three men live out had she been able to have her way. None of the men liked her; all of them declared Ertha to be a little more tolerable than her mother – and a deal more attractive in appearance. In fact, both Chuck and Bevis had pronounced her beautiful, while Dave remained non-committal, preserving his quiet uncommunicative demeanour whenever he happened to be in Gail's company. This particular evening he was strangely brooding, and several odd glances had been sent her way.

'Will you walk with me?' he asked unexpectedly when after dinner Kane went off to his private room. 'I don't expect the Boss will object.'

They were on the verandah, Leta having been put to bed by Gail immediately the meal was finished. Mrs. Farrell and Ertha were also on the verandah, and glances were exchanged between them when Gail rose from her rattan chair and went off into the darkness with Dave.

'Dave,' began Gail when they were some distance from the people on the lighted verandah, 'I do want to apologize for the lies I told you. That's why I've come out with you now, so that I can say I'm sorry for deceiving you.'

'It's not incumbent on you to apologize to me.' He spoke brusquely, walking with some speed so that Gail had to skip now and then in order to keep pace with him.

'That's true. Nevertheless, I am apologizing.'

He turned his head. In the dim light from a half-clouded moon she saw the thin smile that appeared on his mouth.

'It would seem that you want us to be friends?'

83

'Most certainly I do.' They were walking into the bush, taking a path that was stony and narrow. All was still; the immensity of the vast silent spaces was like a world apart from that inhabited by man. It was awesome in its solitude; it held secrets that man would never understand.

Suddenly Dave stopped and stood looking down at her.

'Is there really any need to apologize?' he asked, and Gail, missing the odd inflection in his voice, replied at once,

'Yes, I think so, Dave.'

'I wonder if you understand me. What I'm really asking is . . .' He paused, hesitant for a space, but then making up his mind to speak. 'Are you really Kane's wife?'

She felt her heart jerk, and every nerve-end spring to the alert. So he had made a guess at the truth . . . What must she say? Lies being abhorrent to her she found herself floundering in a maze of uncertainty, asking questions which she had no time to answer. Should she tell him the truth? If she did, would he keep her secret? Also, would he think less of his employer for the deception? Still in a state of mental turmoil, she heard him say, answering his own question for her,

'You're not, Gail,' and he added quickly, 'but Leta is his child.'

She went quite pale, and her throat went dry.

'Dave . . . I . . .'

'You don't know what to say?' Again the thin smile before he added, his tones rather more gentle now, 'That's not unnatural. I've put you in a spot, and you hadn't a Buckley's.'

Diverted for a second, she asked perplexedly,

'What do you mean by that?

'You hadn't a chance. I meant to do it this way – by

84

asking you to come out here with me and then putting the question to you unexpectedly, so that you hadn't an opportunity of preparing an answer.'

It was her turn to smile, a weak smile and quivering, for she was filled with fear now and wished with all her heart that she had not been so eager to come out here so that she could make her apologies to Dave.

'Such a question as you asked would have left me without an answer, no matter under what circumstances it was put to me.'

He made no comment on this statement, but went on to say that although he had made an accurate guess, there was still a good deal he did not understand. He spoke quickly, as if intending to keep her in so confused a state that she would answer his questions before she had time to prevaricate. He had been so shocked at first, he told her, that he was unable even to think, much less realize what had happened. Once he did have time to think, it had not taken him long to deduce that it was all a plan worked out by Kane.

'Reflecting on some of the statements you'd made during our journey here,' he went on, 'I knew for sure that, one: you weren't his wife, and two: that Leta was that "something" you were bringing to Kane. The child's mother – what happened to her?'

'She died.'

'Was Kane married to her?'

Reluctantly she shook her head. It was a strange thing, but she hated the idea that Kane was that sort of man.

'No, he admitted that he wasn't – although Sandra always maintained that she was married to Leta's father.' Dave was looking interrogatingly at her and she thought she might as well tell him everything, for of a surety his intention was to continue questioning her until he had the whole story. When at length she stopped speaking he was shaking his head from side to side, a deep frown etched into his brow.

'It's quite beyond me that the Boss could be like that – that he'd go over to England on holiday and leave a girl with a baby.'

'He didn't know about the baby then.'

'No, so you said, but he isn't the type to let a girl down in the way he appears to have let your cousin down.'

'Appears? He definitely did let her down, and she's dead because of it. Indirectly he's responsible for Sandra's death.'

Thoughtfully he said,

'I don't suppose there can be any mistake . . .?'

'It's strange you should say that. I felt myself that he was an upright man. However, there's no mistake; Sandra knew who the father was – Kane Farrell, the man who owned Vernay Downs Station.'

'He gave her his address, and yet he then left her – just like that, without making any arrangements to see her again. It sounds all phoney to me.'

'There's nothing phoney about it, Dave. Kane's admitted that he's the father of Leta. He's accepted her and intends keeping her, even when I've gone. He also admits that he should have sent Sandra money – when she wrote to him more than four years ago. She told him she had Leta, yet he never did anything to help her.'

Dave looked distressed.

'I had such respect for the Boss,' he said with a frown, 'and such faith too. To have one's faith shattered not only disillusions but it hurts as well.'

She said understandingly,

'I know just how you feel. I don't know him very well and yet I too feel faintly upset that he should be such a rotter, but he is a rotter and you've to accept that he is.'

'I suppose I must,' he owned after a long pause. 'How little we know people!'

'I'm glad it's all cleared up,' she told him with a sudden smile. 'I felt so guilty, so blameworthy.'

He looked at her and responded to her smile.

'I'm glad too, Gail. And because we share this secret I feel close to you—'

'Oh, but . . .' She did not know what to say, because she was unsure of her own feelings towards him. She had already owned that he was the type of man she had always admired, a strong man and rugged . . . but then so was Kane a strong man and rugged, hardened from working outdoors, toughened as a man should be, if he were to be a real man, a truly masculine man.

'Don't say anything yet, Gail,' he pleaded. 'Let's get to know one another, gradually, and pleasantly, as it should be.'

She shook her head.

'We can't become *too* friendly, Dave.'

'Just what does the emphasis mean?' His eyes were on her face and she could not mistake the admiration in them . . . or the expression of hope. 'You're free, Gail, and you have no idea of the weight that was lifted from me after I'd made a guess at the truth.'

She was troubled, even though she knew without doubt that Dave held some sort of attraction for her.

'There are too many obstacles,' she told him. 'Please, Dave, forget about anything beyond mere friendship between us.'

His eyes closely examined her face, taking in the anxiety in the beautiful eyes, the movement of the mouth.

'You've said that you'll be free to leave here once Mrs. Farrell and Ertha have gone. You're going back to England – separating from Kane, for good this time;

this is what he'll spread around in explanation for your departure. This is what you've just told me.'

'I said it was guesswork in the main. Kane must explain why I've gone. And I surmised he'll just make the briefest of explanations. The simplest will be that I can't stand the loneliness and so I've gone away.'

'Leaving your child?'

She shrugged a trifle impatiently.

'There are many difficulties, but they're not my concern. For me – well, I promised to do a job, as it were, by posing as Kane's wife. He's paying me well, but in fairness to myself I must mention that it was Leta's plight that influenced me more than anything else. For if Kane had refused to have her then she would have had to go into a children's home on her arrival back in England. And that would have driven the child to distraction.'

He had to smile, although a little grimly.

'And she would have driven many others to distraction.'

'She isn't improving at all.' Gail was glad that the introduction of Leta had led the conversation on to safer lines.

'She isn't being chastised, so how can she improve?'

'You know why Kane allows her to continue as she is. I'm very sure that when his stepmother has gone then he'll do something about his child.'

'I could do something with her,' he returned musingly. 'There's something about her that attracts me ...' He seemed to be far away – dreaming almost. 'I can't say what it is, but all I know is that I like the kid!'

'You were becoming impatient with her when we were travelling here,' she reminded him with a grimace.

'I agree. But on that sort of a journey one's nerves are never all they should be. There are so many things which can go wrong – such as breakdowns with the car, or someone taking ill. Just supposing one of us *had* taken ill? So you see, Gail, I was not quite myself. But now – well, whenever I'm with Leta I'm strangely happy.' He was in a confiding mood, a young mood that did not seem to fit in with his tough and rugged appearance.

'We must be getting back,' she urged at length. 'We've been out here ages!'

'Yes, indeed we have.' He glanced at his watch; Gail saw the luminous fingers and gave a small gasp.

'Heavens, I didn't think it was that time!'

'Almost ten! Oh, well, there's nothing to hurry for.' And he walked leisurely back to the path which they had left over an hour and a half ago. The distance from the homestead seemed longer than Gail remembered it and she was more than a little agitated when at last they arrived back. Mrs. Farrell was in the sitting-room and her dark and hostile eyes narrowed to mere slits as she said,

'Kane was looking for you, Gail. I told him you and Dave had gone for a walk.' Her eyes strayed significantly to the clock. 'You've been gone for over two hours.'

Gail coloured, much to her annoyance; Dave's face was dark and angry. But he made no comment and Gail realized that he must of course show some respect to the wife of the one-time Boss of Vernay Downs.

'I'm off to bed,' was all he said and, with a smile for Gail, he left the room.

'Kane was not too pleased at your absence.' Mrs. Farrell spoke with undisguised antagonism and her glance was one of contempt as she looked Gail up and down from her head to her feet and back again. 'You and Dave appear to have had plenty to talk about.'

Gail's eyes glimmered.

'Is that a question?' she inquired, adopting the haughty manner which on occasions she found necessary.

The woman shrugged, her mouth curved in a sneer.

'What you and Dave do out there in the darkness has nothing to do with me.' A pause and then with slow deliberation, 'Tongues will wag and scandal flow, but then why should you care? You've been separated from Kane once, so it's more than likely that you'll be separated again.'

'You think so?' The slow but dangerous drawl came from the door, which had been opened silently. Kane stood in the aperture, tall and slim and repelling in the extreme. 'Make no mistake, Rachel, Gail is here for good.'

Again the woman shrugged.

'Time will tell, Kane . . . yes, time will tell.'

'Gail is here for good,' he repeated, coming slowly into the room.

'And so am I,' with a sort of malignant triumph. 'You'll never move me alive, so you can resign yourself to having me here until I die.'

Had he gone a trifle pale? wondered Gail. He was certainly furious beneath that calm exterior.

'You're a thoroughly unpleasant woman,' he said forthrightly. 'You have no place here and you know it—'

'No place? Why, then, did your father make provision for me to remain here? This, he said, was to be my home for as long as I wished to stay.'

'He was infatuated.' Scorn edged the tone. Gail guessed that there had not been a very close relationship between Kane and his father after the marriage had taken place. 'And also, he had no idea of the difficulties he was making for me.'

'If you'd resigned yourself to my being the mistress here, then we'd have got along together much more comfortably.'

'As you're no longer mistress here, then surely it's time for you to accept my offer of another home?'

'It wouldn't be a home like this. I'm used to luxury, Kane, and I'm making sure I don't lower my standard of living by accepting something far smaller and inferior.'

'Smaller, yes. You couldn't expect to live in a place of this size. Inferior – most certainly not!'

'If it's smaller then it's inferior. In any case, the house you offered me is in Sydney, and I don't wish to live there.'

'I said you could choose where you wanted to live, then I'd buy a house for you. The one I offered was for sale and as you came from Sydney and, at first, swore you'd never settle here because of the loneliness, I naturally asked if you'd care for a house in that part of the country.' He shrugged and would have let the matter drop, but his stepmother had a complaint to make.

'I've been meaning to mention this ever since it happened,' she said, throwing a malicious glance at Gail. 'Your – wife cancelled an order of mine which I gave to Miranda. I wanted her to leave what she was doing and tidy out my wardrobes and cupboards, but Miranda thought fit to tell your wife, and the next thing was that my order had been overruled. Gail told Miranda to carry on with what she was doing and then come up to my bedroom. I will not be humiliated in this way with the servants! They've been taking orders from me for some considerable time and I'm not retiring simply because another woman has come to live here!'

'My wife,' he said dangerously. 'Kindly refer to her as that!'

'She shall not override me!' snapped his stepmother, glaring at him. 'I have seniority, if nothing else, and the sooner you both accept this the better it will be for all of us.'

Kane's eyes narrowed ominously.

'Be careful,' he told her softly. 'I'm not a patient man, as you should know.' Mrs. Farrell made no answer and Gail guessed that it was choked-up fury that prevented speech rather than a desire to bring this scene to a close. 'Much as you dislike the idea you've no alternative but to step down now that my wife has arrived. She is the mistress here and as such her orders will always come before yours. In fact, you should already have stopped giving orders at all,' he continued in a firm inflexible tone. 'So I'm telling you now – no more orders from you at all. Keep away from the servants, understand?' His face was set, his eyes hard as the slate they resembled. He was a man of authority, a man commanding, warning, and yet proffering advice.

'The child,' inserted his stepmother defensively, 'do you expect me to tolerate her?'

'My daughter?' His dark brows shot up arrogantly. 'Her place, like that of her mother, is here, in my house!'

'There's something strange about this whole situation,' she murmured, quieter now and looking drawn and tired. 'These two . . .'

Alertly he shot her a glance.

'Well?'

'Nothing,' she replied, and then, rising from the couch on which she was seated, she sent both Gail and Kane baleful looks before sweeping wordlessly from the room.

A few silent moments passed after the door had closed, moments during which Gail's nerves fluttered, for she strongly suspected she was in for a reprimand and, be it ever so mild, she knew she would resent it.

She was right in her suspicions. When presently her 'husband' decided to give her his attention his eyes were glinting in a way which sent ripples of apprehension running along her spine. What a powerful man he was! And what an awe-inspiring personality he possessed! Never had she felt so uncomfortable when in the presence of one of the opposite sex.

'You went out with Dave, I was told?'

'We went for a stroll, yes.'

The grey eyes regarded her disconcertingly.

'You and he were gone for some considerable time.'

'That's correct.'

'What were you doing?'

A hint of anger lit her eyes.

'Walking,' was her brief and rather curt reply.

'All the time?' A narrowed gaze and an attitude of waiting. He might have been a judge, she thought resentfully.

'No, we stopped to talk for a while.'

Kane hesitated, choosing his words with care.

'You heard what Rachel said – that tongues would wag and scandal flow—'

'I didn't take any notice of it. How can scandal flow when there's no ground for scandal?'

'Having been recently reconciled to your husband, you ought not to be strolling in the bush for several hours with another man. Most certainly scandal will flow if this leaks out – which it will, I'm afraid.'

The colour mounted Gail's cheeks, the result both of anger and embarrassment.

'Who can talk – in a place like this?' she wanted to

know. Her nerves were still fluttering, for Kane was stern in his manner and his mouth was set in a thin straight line.

'There are many people who can talk. We have the stockmen and their families, as you very well know. There are the others too – the two schoolteachers, the many other people who make up our community. But besides all these, and much more important as far as my prestige is concerned, there are the other graziers, most of whom are my friends.'

'I thought there were no near neighbours,' she said, diverted. 'Dave tells me that the homesteads in the far Outback are separated by great distances.'

'So they are. But great distances don't trouble us overmuch. My nearest neighbour is thirty miles away. But I have friends whose homesteads are as much as three hundred miles away. We meet from time to time at parties or polo matches or dances. We do have some entertainment,' he added, 'as I think I mentioned to you once before.'

She nodded her head.

'Yes, you did. However, I shouldn't think that my stroll with Dave would reach the ears of people all that way from here.'

'I've just said that it would – or implied that it would. I must ask you, Gail, not to become too friendly with Dave.' Implacable tones which plucked sharply at her temper. All she could think of was that she was doing him a favour, helping him to get rid of two people he did not want in his house. And here he was, ordering and censuring, adopting the most magisterial attitude . . . just as if she were really his wife! She refused to have it and she ventured to tell him this.

'It isn't as if I'm doing anything wrong in walking with him,' she added, speaking swiftly so as not to give

94

him an opportunity of interrupting her. 'I shan't become more friendly than I should, of course, simply because it would not be practical anyway. But as regards your attempting to restrict my movements or control my behaviour – you can be sure that you'll soon discover I've a will of my own.'

An awful silence followed. Gail felt a tightness in her throat and was furious to own that it was the result of fear.

'You appear to forget whom you're speaking to.'

Pale, but determined not to be subdued by the power of him, Gail lifted her chin and replied haughtily,

'And so do you, Kane. I am *not* your wife, and I'd be obliged if you remembered that—' Before she had time to finish a hand was clapped over her mouth, Kane having almost leapt across the room towards her.

'Be quiet!' he hissed furiously. 'Have you no more sense than to say a thing like that! – with ready ears about, as they must be!'

Twisting, she swung out of his grasp.

'I don't believe anyone would stoop to listening at doors!' she retorted.

'I'm taking no chances – mark that!' His face, tight with anger, came close to hers as with an arrogant gesture he again touched her face, this time forcing her head up with a hand under her chin. At the same time he stooped, bending his own head. 'You'll learn to guard your tongue as well as your actions – or there'll be trouble—'

'Just a moment!' Once again she twisted from his grasp, white with fury at being treated in this way. 'You seem to forget—' A flick of his finger cut her short. She watched, fascinated, as with four quick but silent steps he was at the door. Wrenching it open, he then stepped back.

'Were you coming in?' he inquired suavely of his stepmother. 'Have you forgotten something?'

With a face as crimson as the roses in the vase on the table, Mrs. Farrell stuttered and stammered for a few seconds before the door was closed in her face.

'And now do you see what I mean?' from Kane in frigid accents. 'How much she heard I don't know, but I warn you that, should she have learned enough for my plans to have failed, then you can get your belongings packed up – *and* Leta's!' and with that he strode past her and went on to the verandah where, later, she saw him sitting when she looked from her own verandah outside her bedroom window. He was alone, and there was a glass in his hand.

With a deep sigh Gail stepped back, into her room. But she hesitated about closing the window, lest, hearing it, Kane should guess that she might have stepped out on to the verandah above him, and seen him sitting there. Not that it really matters, she thought, but for some strange reason she was reluctant to reveal the fact that he had been in full view of her. She stood for a while, the cool night breeze pleasant on her face. Away in the distance the dark indistinct shapes of animals could be discerned. So still they were, like the age-old hills behind them. She glanced around, into the infinity of space and solitude, remembering that, millions of years ago, this region had been a sea bed, and the mountains would then have been islands. No human had ever set foot upon it, and even now it was untamed land, defiant in the face of man's supreme efforts to bring it under his domination. Fearsome, immense, desolate at this dark hour when the sky and stars seemed to be one with it, and yet she was already affected by its peace, by the unsullied virgin earth, by the total absence of smoke or grime or hideous concrete blocks, or indeed any of those things which man in his haste and greed called 'progress'.

Here, time was way back, with a near-feudal society existing – the lord and his underlings, all living close to nature, where the clear sweet-smelling breeze blew over the spinifex plains where men and cattle roamed, free as the air around them. Some of the men, out on the run, would be away for months at a time, living on 'saddle-pooch tucker' – damper, salt-beef and billy tea. Dave had told her that they loved this nomadic existence, riding from one waterhole to another, often alone for weeks on end, or with Abos for companions. Every so often these lonely stockmen would return to the homestead to report, or to take a well-earned leave, and in the case of Vernay Downs all these men came into the house and were accommodated in comfort until the time when they went off again to roam the wild territory, mustering the cattle.

'There's something about it that gets you,' she murmured to herself when at last she decided to try to close the window quietly and go to bed. 'I'm going to miss it . . .' In her mind came a picture of Dave. Given time he and she could come to that point when he would ask her to marry him. She could then remain here . . . But as she had said to him, there were too many problems. She could not possibly marry Dave and remain here, at Vernay Downs. And it was here that she wanted to stay—

Her thoughts were cut suddenly. Wanted to stay? What a thing to say to herself! She wanted to go home, back to England, to her parents and the new job which she must find. A smile touched her lips as she recalled the letter she had sent to her parents. She had told them that she had accepted an offer of the post of nanny to Leta – and told herself that it wasn't actually an untruth. She could scarcely tell them she was posing as the child's mother, and the wife of her father! She had said that it was the spirit of adventure that had got into her, that the chance of having a few months in Australia was too good to miss. 'I'll be back almost before you've missed me,' she had added confidently, unable to imagine Mrs. Farrell's wanting to remain at Vernay Downs once her authority was taken from her. 'Please phone my boss and give him my sincerest and most humble apologies for leaving so suddenly and without handing in my notice. I expect he'll be angry, and I can't blame him. I shall have to find another post on my return to England. Send out some clothes – just what you think I'll need, and also some books and other personal belongings that you will consider to be useful here, in this wild place so far from civilization.' There had been a little more; she had described Leta's father and added that on the surface, he did not seem the kind of man who would act in so dastardly a manner as he had towards Sandra.

Gail knew what kind of reply she would receive. Her parents, as she had told Kane, had never interfered in her decisions. She was old enough and level-headed enough to be able to keep out of danger, they would say – this after declaring she was quite mad to think she could manage that dreadful child – that she must please herself, but they would be glad when she returned to the fold, as it were. Her mother would say little about the job her daughter had lost, but she would secretly assert that Gail would never find such another, no matter how hard she looked. She had short hours and long holidays, this because her boss was himself working fewer hours than normal, as he was sort of semi-retired yet spending some of his time at the office.

'Bless them both,' said Gail as after taking a shower she got into bed. 'How very simple they make things for me; how uncomplicated it is not to have them inter-fere.' She snuggled down and reached to pull the silken cord which would plunge the room into darkness. Less than five minutes later she was asleep.

CHAPTER SIX

Just a fortnight later the letter arrived, delivered by the mail plane which landed on Kane's own airstrip. She was reading it when Kane came into the room, dusty and hot from a hard day's riding, and not in the best of moods either, having just been told that three of his best Abo stockmen had gone 'walkabout', that is, gone into the bush where they would live native until, tired of the life, they would return and ask for their jobs back. Mistakenly surmising that his stare was an interrogating one, Gail explained that the letter was from her parents.

'I told them that I'd accepted a post as nanny to Leta,' she began, when the look in his eyes stopped her from proceeding any further.

'Will you never learn to be careful?' he asked with an acid bite to his tone. 'You should have been warned by what happened the other night. You know full well that my stepmother is not above listening at doors!'

Gail bit her lip.

'I'm sorry,' she said in a subdued voice. 'I just can't get used to the idea that anyone would be so dishonourable as to listen at a door.'

'What have your people to say?' he asked in a less hostile tone. 'I was told that you received a parcel.'

'Mother sent me one or two things. The rest are coming later.' She glanced down at the letter and added with a grimace, 'Mother's accepted my decision, as I said she would.' Soft the words and also Gail had automatically moved closer to Kane. She was aware then of his great height, for she was forced to tilt her head right back in order to look into his face. Sweatbegrimed, it was nevertheless still handsome. 'Perhaps you'd like to read it for yourself?' she invited, amazing herself by the offer. She was puzzled that she could treat Kane like this; she wanted only to retain the contempt – and to reveal it now and then, just so that he would be reminded of what he had done to her cousin. Instead, she was as time passed becoming almost eager to be pleasant with him, and to have him be pleasant with her.

'Not just now,' he returned. 'I must go and have a bath.'

'Of course. Later, then?'

He nodded, looking at her with an odd expression.

'Very well, seeing that you obviously want me to. Put it on the table in my sitting-room.' He turned, frowning, as Ertha entered the room. She was dressed for dinner and Gail had to admit that there was a most attractive beauty about the girl. It would not have been surprising had Kane fallen in love with her. Perhaps, decided Gail, Ertha would have stood a much better chance if her mother had not made an enemy of Kane. Mrs. Farrell had not been very clever, but the more she learned about her the more Gail realized that it was the woman herself who wanted to rule at Vernay Downs and that although she would have preferred her daughter to be the mistress rather than another girl, she would still have resented to a large degree anyone who superseded her.

'Ah, Kane, so you're back!' Mrs. Farrell followed Ertha into the room. 'That child—'

'You mean, my daughter?'

'Leta! She's insulted me for the whole of this day!'

'Leta's been at school,' interrupted Gail with a frown, 'so how can she have troubled you all day?' Gail sent a look towards Kane who, from the first, had insisted that Leta attend the school where provision was made for the acceptance of children from the age of four years. 'She's in bed now—'

'Is she? And she's been at school, you say? That brat's played truant this afternoon!'

'Are you sure?' Kane's stern voice boded ill for Leta, should what his stepmother have said prove to be true. 'Gail, didn't you notice her about?'

She shook her head, feeling guilty.

'I've been upstairs, helping Daisybell with the preparation of the guest-rooms. You said we'd need them when we had my party.'

'I'll get to the bottom of this,' he began, obviously intending to go up to Leta and question her. But Ertha intervened, supporting her mother's statement.

'She's been dodging about, trying to hide one minute and the next going out of her way to torment Mother.' She spoke quietly, but the malice in her tones was plainly portrayed.

'Why didn't one of you inform Gail of this?'

'We didn't know where she was,' replied Ertha, smooth as oil as she looked up at him and added, 'It was Dave's afternoon off and we thought that perhaps Gail had gone off somewhere with him.'

Flushing vividly, Gail opened her mouth to protest, and then decided that to defend herself would only result in further embarrassment for her, and also for Kane. That he was furious was revealed in the drifts of crimson which had appeared at the sides of his mouth. What he would have said was never known because Mrs. Farrell came in with the sly and subtle reminder that he had forbidden her to interfere either with what Gail was doing, or what Leta was doing.

'I did have an idea that Gail was with Daisybell,' she continued, 'but after all the arguments we've been having lately, Kane, I felt I mustn't bring Gail away from the task she had chosen – even though that task was quite unnecessary; we have two other lubras who could have assisted Daisybell with the guest rooms.'

Kane shot her a glowering look, and turned away towards the door. But at that moment it opened and Leta stood there, fully dressed.

'I don't want to go to bed,' she said, coming into the room. 'I'm not tired, so I want to stay up for dinner.'

'You chose tomorrow—'

'I've changed my mind. I'm staying up tonight!' She was in one of her most intractable moods, and had it been left to Gail Leta would undoubtedly have got her own way. But Kane, already in a temper, was clearly intending to stand no nonsense. It was the first time he had adopted an attitude of such firmness with her, and Gail guessed that she was in for a surprise.

'Come here,' he ordered sharply, and Leta gave a small start. 'I said – *come here!*'

Leta obeyed, but dragged her feet across the thick-pile carpet. Gail glanced at Mrs. Farrell, and then at Ertha. Both their faces revealed the intense dislike they felt for the child. In all fairness Gail could not blame them, since Leta had harassed them unbearably at times.

'Daddy—' began Leta, but she was not allowed to say any more.

'Where were you this afternoon?'

'At school, of course,' came the immediate and innocent reply. Kane's eyes narrowed, but Leta looked up at him with that expression of defiant unconcern which had always been so familiar to Gail and, indeed, to all who had known the child. Undoubtedly she had a strong, forceful character – just like her father, thought Gail, looking from one to the other and trying to find some physical likeness, as she had done several times before. She found none . . . not one line or feature that could be said was peculiar to both father and daughter.

'I said this afternoon, not this morning.'

'I was at school all day. Ask Miss MacKay.' So bland her manner, and Gail could scarcely believe she was telling a lie.

'Very well, we shall do just that.' Keenly he watched his daughter's face. Gail saw no change in her expression, but Kane obviously did, which said much for his powers of observation. 'Come with me; we'll go over to her bungalow.' That he had no intention of doing so was without doubt. It was a long way to the bungalows, and Kane was already tired and dirty from his work outdoors, work that had to be done though the heat had shimmered over the plains like a haze of white-hot vapour.

'Well . . .' began Leta, screwing up her face as if the prospect of seeing her teacher was highly distasteful to her. 'I did come home early, Daddy, because I had a headache.' The last words came brightly and it was plain that the excuse had come to her unexpectedly.

Kane said nothing; he was obviously saving any reprimand for later, when his stepmother was not present.

'Very well, Leta. And now you can go to bed.'

'You're allowing her to get away with it!' gasped Mrs. Farrell. 'And what about her rudeness to me?'

'I wasn't rude! I only said you looked like an ape, and that was the truth, so how can it be rude?'

'Leta!' Gail could not allow that to pass. Horrified, she took a step towards Leta, intending to give her a shake. But Kane's finger was lifted and Gail stopped in her tracks.

'Normal child development,' he said. 'If Rachel can't understand this then it's entirely her own fault. I am not willing to put a rein on what is natural.' So cool . . . but Gail was staring perceptively at him. Mrs. Farrell also knew what he was doing, as her next words revealed.

'You'll get tired before I do, Kane. Don't forget – I know you well enough to be able to predict a speedy end to your daughter's disgraceful conduct. For you're the very last one to tolerate such disregard for politeness –and authority.'

Undoubtedly this was true, and as he was not willing to deny it Kane changed the subject and with a return to his customary calm and languid drawl he told Leta to go to bed.

'I'm not tired; I've said it once.' She sat down on a chair and swung her legs. 'Why doesn't Mrs. Farrell keep her back straight? My teacher at play-school said that all people should keep their backs straight because you get a hump if you don't. That's why you look like an ape—'

'Leta, that's enough!' It was Gail who spoke and she was deliberately avoiding Kane's eyes. 'You've gone too far! Now, apologize to Mrs. Farrell and then off you go to bed! I've had quite sufficient of you for one evening!'

Silence. Although sensing his anger Gail still refused to look at Kane. And she was not allowing Leta to have any more of her own way. If Kane should decide to allow her to stay up for dinner then she, Gail, would oppose him.

'You mean, say I'm sorry?'

'That's exactly what I mean.'

'I never say I'm sorry, because I'm not sorry!'

Still Kane remained impassive, an interested on-looker, nothing more. Surprised, but too occupied with Leta to waste time finding a reason for his conduct, Gail told Leta once again to apologize. There was a battle, Leta giving cheek, as Gail knew she would. But she was quite determined to make her go to bed, and as once again it looked as if Leta would win Gail turned in desperation to Kane. He nodded instantly in answer to her unspoken plea and, lifting Leta bodily, he carried her, kicking and screaming, from the room.

Gail was ready for bed when she heard the gentle knock on the door connecting her room with that of Kane. Snatching a pretty — but not very practical — negligé she flung it on and opened the door.

'May I come in?' Amusement lit the grey eyes as the colour mounted Gail's cheeks. She was fidgeting nervously with the tie at the waist of the negligé; it was a wide ribbon and in her haste to fasten it she had managed to get it knotted.

'Yes, of course.' He was in anyway, she thought, already behind him as he stopped in the centre of the room. 'Is it something important?'

He was fully dressed, attractive in a tropical suit and light green shirt. She had seen Ertha, at dinner, sending him glance after glance, and Gail could not but be a little sorry for her, as she must be dreadfully put out by the appearance of his wife.

'I just wanted to put your mind at rest regarding what happened before dinner. You seemed anxious that I'd be annoyed at your interference?'

'I was anxious,' she admitted freely, her hands still occupied with the knot. 'But on the other hand, I was determined not to allow Leta to go to any further lengths than she already had.' Gail was angry at his coolness, at the way he turned a blind eye to all of his daughter's disgraceful behaviour. And her anger, as always, lent her courage. 'While on the one hand I understand your reasons for neglecting to chastise Leta, I feel that there should be limits beyond which she ought not to be allowed to go – this for her own good as much as for the comfort of others in the house. She flaunts every single rule of courtesy and respect – and you ignore it! She knows that there's some reason for it, since she's so highly intelligent.' He made to interrupt, but she continued swiftly, 'Sandra did at least try, but you're just making the child worse!' Anger had always enhanced her eyes, so her mother had said, and now Kane was looking down at her with an odd expression on his face. He was absorbed, it would appear, and she did wonder if he had taken in all she had been saying. She was soon to know, for, having brought his attention from her eyes, he looked her up and down and said,

'I believe I've already warned you about your lack of respect when talking to me.'

'And I reminded you that you are not my husband.' She spoke sharply but quietly, this time remembering his warning about people listening at doors. 'You can't dictate to me, Kane, and the sooner you accept that the better.' She was pale now, and her hands had dropped to her sides. For some strange unfathomable reason this strained unfriendly atmosphere troubled her. It almost hurt, in fact, in some way that both disturbed and angered her. Why was harmony so important? She was doing a job – no more than that. And when it was completed she would leave Vernay Downs behind her for ever, and Leta too. Kane Farrell's face would fade from her memory; the day would come when all this was vague and indistinct – an image in the distant past that would reappear only at intervals, when something happened to remind her of it.

Kane said, deliberately and very softly,

'I hate to remind you, Gail, that I was not married to Leta's mother—'

'What has that to do with it!'

'Allow me to finish!' he snapped. 'What I was going to say was that I have no need to keep her here with me.'

'I see . . .' She spoke after a long silence. 'So you're holding over my head the fact that you could, at any time you like, send Leta away?'

'I could order you to take her away.'

Subdued yet furious, Gail lowered her eyes, and automatically began fidgeting with the knot again. What must she do? Her pride urged her to adopt a careless attitude, to treat with contempt his threat. But what about Leta? She would feel the wrench were she to be taken from here now. By some miracle she had managed – for the first time in her life – to get along with other children, having made friends with Marion, the five-year-old daughter of one of the stockmen, and Gerald, the son of one of the rouseabouts. Also, she was extremely fond of Kane, despite her tantrums of this evening when he had carried her forcibly to her room, and kept her there by the simple means of locking her door. She liked Dave – and not only because he was teaching her to ride a horse; she got on tolerably well with the three lubras, and Daisybell went so far as to make her biscuits twice a week, cutting them into the shapes of animals and birds.

'I promised Sandra I'd bring her to you,' said Gail at last, her voice low and devoid of any hint of anger. 'I've kept the promise, but – but if you send Leta away again . . .' Distressed now, she looked up at him, into those hard grey eyes, eyes which seemed to be measuring her darkly as they moved, with a sort of slow precision, to the hands that were occupied with the knotted ribbon.

'Let me help you.' The offer came spontaneously, and judging by his expression it surprised Kane as much as it surprised her. 'You've been struggling ever since I came in here.'

'It — it doesn't matter . . .' Why should she be so close to tears? Could it be for the most absurd reason that he had said something to ease the tension? 'I c-can manage it.'

'But I'll manage it far easier from here.' And, bending down, he took her hands away and proceeded to unfasten the knot. She watched his bent head, noting the thick and healthy hair, the strength of the neck, the broadness of the shoulders. But what she was profoundly conscious of was the presence of his hands, so close to her that she could feel their warmth. A sense of breathlessness, of inexplicable excitement pervaded her body and she was aware also of a curious constriction of her throat. Her mind, too, seemed to be affected, with thoughts refusing to be marshalled. And when at length Kane straightened up she was blushing adorably, and her eyes were oddly bewildered as they met his half puzzled, half amused stare. 'There,' he said, leaving her to tie the bow, 'it's done!'

'Thank you,' she murmured, her lashes coming down, for his amusement appeared to be growing with every second that passed. It embarrassed her and in a sort of defensive move she mentioned the reason for his coming into her room.

'Yes,' he said, 'it was merely to tell you that your attitude was the correct one. As Leta's mother you must at times assert your authority.'

She stared at him in surprise.

'I fully expected you'd resent my interference,' she told him. 'After all, I'm not her mother — but you are her father, so it would have been natural if you'd resented it . . .' Slowly her words tapered off to silence, because of the odd expression that had entered his eyes, and because of the inexplicable twitching of his lips and the slight shaking of his head which, she decided, was mechanical, a gesture of which he himself was scarcely aware. 'Have I said something to amuse you?' she asked, totally fascinated by his manner. 'You're laughing at me?' she added accusingly.

Kane shook his head.

'Not at you, my dear ... at something you said, though. However, do continue with what you were telling me.'

'Won't you say what it was that amused you?'

Again he shook his head, this time a little more firmly.

'Carry on with what you were saying,' he invited again, and Gail with a shrug of her shoulders went on to say that, having always regarded herself as Leta's aunt rather than her second cousin, she felt she had a certain right to assert some authority, but repeated that she would have understood had Kane resented her interference.

'When the time comes for me to take her in hand,' he said reflectively, 'I shall not require your help, nor will I be happy if you should interfere. However, the time is not yet; we are acting parts, you and I, and we must remember this – all the time. Had you not asserted your authority it would have looked very strange indeed. My stepmother is no fool; in fact, she's as astute a woman as I've ever met,' he added with a grim note to his voice.

'She knows what you're about, that's for sure.'

'And to be expected. As she said, I'm the last one to tolerate a disregard for authority – especially my authority,' he added, and his expression was such that a slight shudder passed down Gail's spine.

'She also predicted that you'd become tired before she would.'

At this his lips curved in a sneer.

'We shall see about that. I have a great capacity for

patience—'

'You have?' she broke in without a moment's thought. 'I wouldn't have thought so—' And then she stopped, aghast at what she had said.

'Isn't it a little early for you to make an assessment of my character?' he inquired dryly. 'After all, I estimate that we've spent no more than three hours a day in one another's company – that's an average, of course.'

'It has never struck me how little time we've had on our own,' she returned, aware only after the words had been uttered that this was perhaps not the right way of putting it. However, he made no sign that she had either amused or surprised him and she continued by adding, as tactfully as she could, that he had not struck her as a very patient man.

'I don't suffer fools gladly, if that's what you mean,' he said. 'However, I believe you misunderstood my meaning. When I implied that I had patience I really meant that if it's to be a waiting game then I'll have more staying power than Rachel.'

'I see.' Gail nodded her head. 'I did misunderstand you. But in any case,' she went on with a sudden smile, 'I spoke impulsively, didn't I?'

He made no answer to this, appearing to have become rather more than a little interested in her expression. Her lips were still parted slightly, her eyes still bright from the tears that had come so close to falling. Her lovely hair, gleaming from the brushing it had just received, shone in the shaded light from the bedside lamp; her slender body was swaying very slightly, so that the negligé, its tie forgotten, swung open to reveal alluring curves tantalizingly veiled by the folds of a diaphanous white nylon nightdress.

His eyes gave away the fact that he was admiring the picture she made and with a swift movement she snatched together the edges of the negligé, her colour rising in the most enchanting way, and her long thick eyelashes fluttering down as, in her embarrassment, she avoided his gaze. Kane laughed softly and unexpectedly and she glanced up. His mouth was now lifting at the corners, portraying his amusement. She caught her breath, in a curious manner which produced an access of suffocation ... and a feeling of expectancy. A little dazed by these sensations, she could only wonder vaguely at them, the only explanation emerging being that when he smiled like that the attraction was such that she was unable to ignore it.

Gail continued to stare; Kane remained motionless in the centre of the room, his back to the window. It was a moment of profound tension with the very air vibrating around them. Behind Kane the moon was visible through the uncurtained window, an enormous moon, full, and shining like polished silver. It had risen behind the mountains, but now its light fell upon the foothills leaving the high hollows bathed in shadow. The night was soft in its gentle beams; the plains drowsed lazily in their splendid solitude. Vast land! – immense, lonely and withdrawn as some mighty god on his golden throne.

Yet there was magic in the aspect of moonlit plains, in the optical illusion of a tilted sky, in the stars of the southern hemisphere, in the secrecy that lay tantalizingly beyond the range of vision.

'I th-think you'd better go,' she stammered at last, quite unable to think of anything else to say. 'It's getting l-late.'

He glanced at his watch and said,

'You're quite right, Gail, it's getting late. Good night ... my dear.'

Why the hesitation? She thought about it and suddenly she knew that he had almost left out the 'my', saying only, 'dear'.

Dear ... She swallowed hard. His manner thrilled her in some delicious kind of way; it seemed to tempt, to beckon, to entice ...

What madness was this? With determination she gave herself a mental shake, but at that moment Kane smiled ...

'You must go,' she repeated, and this time there was an urgency in her tone of which she was oddly ashamed. It should not be there simply because there should be no need for it! Need ... She swallowed again and turned her face away from him, afraid of what he might see there. She did not know herself, but she was still afraid, for every nerve in her body was tingling, affected by her desire to draw closer to him. Her heart throbbed wildly so that she felt an almost physical discomfort within her.

'It's almost midnight,' she told him in a high-pitched tone of voice. 'I'm tired – and – and I'm s-sure you are too!'

A twitching of his lips; a glance that took in the bright eyes, the quivering mouth, the little clenched fists and the slight heaving of her breasts.

'Yes, Gail,' he returned softly, 'I am rather tired.' He said good night again and then he was gone, and she was staring with a fascinated gaze at the closed door, half expecting it to open again and for Kane to come back into her room.

There was no lock. Up till now this had not troubled her, but suddenly it was a thing of importance ... it was a danger. Tomorrow she would see him about having the door locked. It was just that the key was missing – or perhaps it was on his side.

'It must be on my side! I shall insist! In any case, an unlocked door between us isn't the thing at all, and I should have done something about it right at the beginning.'

Even after she got into bed she was staring at the door, afraid to put out the light. But inevitably sleep claimed her and, drowsy and on the very borders of slumber, she extinguished the light.

The following morning she missed him and as the first opportunity was in the evening after she had washed and changed, she knocked on his door, after hearing him moving about in his room.

'Come in,' he called, but she merely opened the door and stood looking in at him. 'Something I can do for you?' He seemed flippant, she thought, eyeing him with some suspicion. All day she had been thinking about what he had done to Sandra; all day she had been admitting that there was something so incredibly attractive about him that there was every excuse for her cousin. And in between these thoughts and conclusions had intruded the fact that she herself might be in danger. Never had she dreamed that a man could affect her in the way Kane had affected her last night, but it was there and she was honest enough to admit that it was there. Temptation ... and a man who had already let one girl down.

'Yes, Kane, there is something you can do for me.' She hoped she sounded brisk and unemotional. 'I've been thinking; it isn't the thing for this door to be unlocked. So I'm asking you to let me have the key. I see that the lock is quite old – you don't find brass ones nowadays – so if the key is lost perhaps you'll have a new lock fitted?'

The grey eyes flickered over her, a veiled expression in their depths. Was he amused again? she wondered.

'What has caused you to think of this?' he queried. 'You've been here over three weeks and you've never bothered about it before.'

She swallowed hard.

'It's just that it occurred to me today that it isn't quite right—'

'Today?' with a hint of satire. 'Or ... could it have been last night?'

Gail coloured vividly. So he knew! She stepped back instinctively, desiring only to escape from this man's all-seeing eyes.

'The lock,' she stammered, 'I w-want it – and at once!'

Kane had been brushing his hair when she opened the door and he now tapped the back of the brush on his hand in a thoughtful gesture.

'I'm afraid a locked door is impossible,' was his cool rejoinder. 'We are married, remember?'

'*Supposed* to be married!'

'That's what I meant. And so we can scarcely have a locked door between us, especially as we've just become reconciled after a long and distant separation.'

'I want it locked!'

'I've said it's impossible.'

'I insist! No one will know—'

'The lubras will know!'

'Do they matter?'

'Not particularly. But my stepmother is bound to find out, and then—' He spread a hand expressively. 'I've warned you, Gail, that we have to be careful.'

'I can't see that Mrs. Farrell can find out!' Gail glared at him defiantly. 'I intend having this door locked, so you can have it seen to tomorrow!'

Only then did Kane's manner change. Gone was the humour, the hint of understanding that had underlain his words up till now. His eyes took on a steely look; his whole attitude was one of arrogance and implacability.

'The door will not be locked,' he told her. 'And now, if you don't mind, I'd like to finish what I was doing.' Icy the tone and dark his expression. She stood there, defiant still and yet hesitant about continuing the argument. But if she allowed him to have the last say then she would live in perpetual fear.

'I must have it locked – I *must*!'

'Gail,' he said, very softly, 'I've told you several times that it remains unlocked – No, don't interrupt me! My word is law in this house and you, like everyone else, will respect it. Do I now make myself clear?'

'What you're telling me is that you, as supreme master of this establishment – of this vast estate – have the right to give me orders – and that I must obey them!' Possessed now of a burning vapour of fury, she did make some endeavour to guard her tongue a little, but she failed and, speaking without sufficient consideration, she looked at him directly and said,

'You seem to have forgotten what you did to Sandra! If you think I'm intending to run any risks then you're mistaken!'

'Sandra!' The one word was snapped out; his eyes looked smoulderingly into hers. 'How dare you mention her! And as for risks—' Disdainfully his glance swept her figure. 'My girl, you have no appeal whatsoever for me!' Veins stood out on his temples but, unlike Gail, he was able to control his wrath and his voice was quiet as he repeated, 'No, appeal whatsoever.'

'I'm relieved to hear it,' returned Gail in a choked voice. It was a tame response, but she could think of nothing else to say; she was unable to think clearly, consumed as she was by anger. She would not have her way, though. That fact did stand out clearly in her mind. She retreated, backing into her bedroom and closing the door. And suddenly she was in tears, all anger dissolved in self-pity. She wanted nothing more than to go home, away from this unfriendly house with its hostile women, its fractious child, and its arrogant, overbearing master.

CHAPTER SEVEN

SHE awoke before the first hint of dawn had touched the mountains. Drowsily she turned on to her back, yawning luxuriously. How still ... how silent . ᴢ ᴢ It was like another world, this tough and fearsome land to which she had come, bringing the child to her father. What quirk of fate had caused her to stay? Would she still have come had she had any inkling of what was in store for her? Impossible to answer so difficult a question, and yet, as into her thought-stream there intruded that moment when her promise to Sandra had been made, Gail rather suspected that she would have been most reluctant to go back on that promise. 'Fate is fate,' her grandmother used to say when Gail as a young teenager visited her every Saturday afternoon, 'and it's no use trying to steer yourself out of its way. It's all-powerful because what it brings was ordained, long before you were born, before your pretty eyes opened to the light of day. Never do battle against it, my dear. It'll be both futile and frustrating.'

Good advice, because fate was all-powerful, but sometimes one felt that, if only one had acted differently, then fate could have been thwarted. Gail sat up in bed and put on the light. Four-thirty! But she knew what was wrong; it was that scene last night that, having been on her mind, caused her to wake before her time. With an automatic movement she turned again, to face the door. And she frowned heavily. She would never feel safe while it remained unlocked. Why, Kane could enter her room at any time of the day or night, should he choose to do so! It was a strange circumstance that she had never felt unsafe until the

night before last. She had known the door was unlocked, but somehow the fact had not registered firmly
enough for it to worry her. Recalling her own
emotional condition, brought on by the man's devas-
tating good looks and arresting personality, she was left
in no doubt as to the origin of her fears. Nevertheless,
she shirked an admission that it was herself she feared
rather than Kane Farrell. She reminded herself over
and over again of what had befallen poor Sandra ...
and as she had said to Kane last night, she had no
intention of suffering a similar fate.

Colour rose swiftly as she went over that particular
part of the scene enacted in her bedroom last evening.
So scornfully he had raked her with those hard
grey eyes, assuring her in no uncertain terms that she
held no attraction for him at all. Well, she had no wish
to hold any attraction for him! He was the very last
man she could fall for and in consequence she had no
wish that he should become interested in her as a
woman.

The dawn broke at last and Gail rose, going to the
window and pulling aside the curtains. It was almost
five o'clock and the sun was coming up, spraying the
mountainsides with gold. It was a breathtaking sight
and one Gail had seen on a couple of occasions before.
In no time at all the sun was white and blinding, but
a blue-white mist still clung to the mountain summits
and drifted about in the hollows lower down. The mob
of cattle grazed on the slopes, their shapes dark against
green hillsides. Away in another direction the aspect
was one of endless miles of spinifex country, with the
dry creek bed winding about, its banks dotted with
unwieldy gum trees which seemed always to be shedding their barks. Closer to, the yellow balls of candyfloss
– flowers of the wattle trees – were transformed to gold
as the sun's rays caught them.

She glanced down; the sun had filtered the ornamental trees in the garden, creating a mosaic of light and shade which spread across the lawn to the wide verandah directly beneath her window. She stiffened slightly as a figure emerged – Kane, dressed in tight-fitting jeans and a slouch hat. He stood there, by the rail, staring out over his domain. She wished she could see his expression, and then the next moment she was asking herself why she should be interested. Was he looking with pride at all he saw? She took it for granted that his customary arrogance would be there in his eyes, and in the set of his mouth. An estate as large as a county . . . . It was almost unbelievable! There must be numerous parts that he had never even seen, and it was there that the nomadic stockmen roamed, over the wild places, content with the freedom that was theirs. Her eyes wandering from the man below, Gail saw movement going on among the bungalows on the hill. Everyone rose early, and soon the homestead kitchen would be rowdy with big men who had come in to eat big meals of porridge, eggs and chunks of fresh beef.

Kane moved and her eyes rested on his figure again, something quite indefinable stirring her senses as the moments passed. She watched his lithe and slender figure as he went towards the home paddock where his horse was being rubbed down by one of the rouseabouts. A moment later, and with the ease of an acrobat, he swung on to its back and rode away towards the hills. Magnificent, both man and beast! She envied Kane, in a way, for he was so skilled and proud and so confident. But then he was rather like a king here, ruling over this stupendous estate. It would have been strange indeed had he not been proud and confident.

She was about to turn into the room when the jackos began to send forth their infectious morning laughter.

Gail stood watching them, perched on the end of a branch, chuckling joyfully. They would stop now and then, their heads cocked as they looked down, alert for the appearance of an unwary lizard or mouse that might make a tasty meal. These birds ate worms and grubs only when they could not get anything else, Dave had told her. A couple of magpies appeared and one of the jackos swooped to give one an unfriendly jab, then he flew back to his perch, laughing triumphantly.

At last Gail turned away and after washing and dressing she went down to the breakfast-room expecting to find Leta already there, probably tormenting one of the lubras.

'Where's Leta?' she asked Daisybell, equally surprised by Daisybell's presence as by Leta's absence.

'She's unwell, and Miranda's looking after her, that's why I'm here, seeing to the table.' She looked harassed, and Gail told her to go back to the kitchen and attend to the men's requirements.

'I'll go up to Leta,' she ended and, with a grateful nod, Daisybell left the room.

Leta was sitting up in bed drinking tea. But as Gail entered she turned on an expression of pain.

'My stomach!' she groaned before Gail could speak. 'Oh, I'm in agony!'

Gail looked at Miranda and her mouth tightened. The lubra was under no illusions either, but Leta with her forcefulness had demanded attention with such arrogance and authority that the poor woman had offered little or no resistance.

'You can go back to your work,' Gail told her quietly. 'I'll attend to my daughter.'

'Thank you, Mrs. Farrell – I was very busy when the little miss called me—'

'I understand,' broke in Gail. 'There's no need to explain.'

When the door had closed Gail gave her full attention to the child.

'I'm ill!' declared Leta belligerently on noting Gail's expression. 'I can't go to school with these pains in my stomach!'

'I don't believe you've any pains at all!' With a determined gesture she took the cup and saucer from Leta's hand. And then she flung back the bedclothes. 'Come on, up you get!'

'I won't—' Leta began to scream so loudly that it was impossible for her not to be heard in the next bedroom, which happened to be that of Mrs. Farrell. Within seconds she was in Leta's room, a dressing-gown flung over her nightdress.

'What on earth's all the noise about?' she demanded furiously. 'I was asleep—'

'At this time?' interrupted Leta rudely. 'You should be having your breakfast now – you always do have it early!'

'Oh . . . !' quivered the woman, turning to glower at Gail. 'Are you going to stand there and allow her to speak to me like this?'

Gail was losing colour rapidly. Nothing would have afforded her more satisfaction than to smack Leta, hard. But she knew she dared not, because of what her father would say. He wanted his stepmother to be treated in this way; it was all part of the plan.

Gail sighed; she was fast beginning to tire of the whole business; she was also troubled about Leta, and the effect on her of having not an atom of discipline from anyone in the house.

'Kane will talk to her,' answered Gail at last, and was not surprised when Mrs. Farrell told her not to be ridiculous, that Kane would actually approve of Leta's conduct.

'I shall take the law into my own hands,' she threatened. 'I shall thrash the creature! I'll put a stop to this scheme of my stepson's!'

'If you touch me,' warned Leta in a loud voice, and having forgotten all about her pains, 'I'll bite you and kick you! And my daddy will hit you as well!'

'Be quiet!' commanded Gail. 'And do as I tell you! Get up at once; you're going to be late for school.'

'I'm not going to school—' Leta began groaning again. 'I'm dying! I want the Flying Doctor!'

'Ah . . .' Gail's eyes widened perceptively. 'Dave told you about the Flying Doctor. I heard him. And so you want us to bring him out here, do you?'

'She'd do that?' gasped Mrs. Farrell. 'She'd bring the doctor out, just for a stupid little pain?'

'Little pain!' cried Leta, rising now as if preparing to carry out her threat of a few minutes ago. 'It's a big pain! I'm dying, I said!'

'What's all this?' From the open doorway Kane's languid voice was heard and all three heads turned in his direction. 'Leta, did I hear you say you were ill?'

'Oh . . . Daddy, I'm dying with pain!' Leta went towards him with slow, agonizing footsteps. 'Send for the doctor – please! Mummy isn't listening to me!'

Her full attention on his face, Gail gave him a challenging look. Impassively he received this, saying slowly to his stepmother,

'You can go, Rachel. There's no necessity for any interference from you.'

'She said she'd beat me,' cried Leta, managing to produce actual tears. 'Don't let her, Daddy—'

'Rachel, I told you to leave us!' Undoubtedly he was angry now, and there was a granite-like quality about his expression. 'I can't see what you're doing in here anyway.'

'She was screaming fit to waken the dead! I'd stayed in bed, resting because I had a headache, and was disturbed by this deafening scream—'

'All right – all right,' with impatience but also control. 'Go back, then, and take your rest.'

After she had flounced from the room Gail turned on Kane and regardless of his narrowed eyes and darkling expression she told him firmly that she was not willing for this present state of affairs to continue.

'There's nothing at all wrong with Leta,' she added wrathfully, 'and if you pander to her on this occasion I shall not support you!'

An awful silence followed; Kane was already having difficulty with his temper and Gail's defiant announcement served only to produce white drifts of fury at the corners of his mouth.

'Firstly, I haven't given any indication that I'm intending to pander to her! Secondly – secondly, Gail,' he said in harsh implacable tones, 'you'll please remember who I am!' Three swift strides having brought him close, he towered above her, menacing in his attitude, his sun-bitten face tight with anger.

'What about my pains?' began Leta when, slowly swinging his long body round, Kane looked down at her, his eyes narrowed and glinting.

'Get dressed,' he ordered, 'and be sharp about it. You're going to school – and without your breakfast!'

Leta stared unbelievingly at him, her face slowly taking on a purple hue as her uncontrollable temper rose to take possession of her.

'I've got pains—!'

'Get dressed!' thundered Kane and, as on a previous occasion, he lifted her bodily and dumped her in the bathroom. His hand on her shoulder kept her from turning to run out again, but in her fury she did no more than dig her teeth into his finger. But it was a mistake; Kane took her over his knee and the screams she had uttered before were nothing to those that issued from her lips now. 'Gail, wash her hands and face,' he ordered curtly, putting the child back on her feet, 'and then help her to get dressed.'

'I won't . . .' But Leta's voice weakened under the threatening stare of her father and without more ado – but crying loudly still – she allowed herself to be made ready for school. 'I'm hungry—'

'Off you go! If you run you'll be early. If you're late you get another spanking when you come home!'

'It's about time you did that,' Gail could not help saying as, standing by the window she watched Leta racing across the lawn towards the path along which she had to go in order to reach the school. 'It's utter nonsense to allow her to continue as she has been doing. She'll have everyone's nerves on edge if she isn't controlled.'

His smouldering gaze was transferred to her.

'I've already warned you twice about the manner in which you speak to me. If you continue to ignore those warnings it'll be the worse for you.' He looked arrogantly at her, noting her flushed face and the defiant light in her eyes. 'If my plan doesn't show some sign of working within the next week or two, then we'll talk about your going back to England, and taking that child with you—!' He stopped, but Gail with her quick intelligence saw at once that he had cut the words because he considered he had made a mistake.

'That child?' she repeated slowly. 'Isn't that an odd sort of way to talk about your daughter?'

'Does it never occur to you that, not having seen Leta before, I have difficulty in becoming accustomed to the fact that she's my own child?' He had calmed down somewhat and he had also turned his head, as if he would conceal his expression from her.

Gail made no comment on this, but returned to what

he had first said.

'If you send Leta and me away your stepmother and Ertha — and in fact, everyone, is going to ask questions which you're going to find difficult to answer.'

The grey eyes glinted again.

'That,' he told her curtly, 'is my affair. It need not concern you.'

She said tightly,

'You promised that, if I agreed to stay here, you'd keep Leta. Are you intending to go back on that promise, then?'

'If you continue to treat me with disrespect then I shall consider I have grounds for going back on my promise. When I made it I didn't bargain for this attitude of yours, which,' he added slowly and with a sort of harsh emphasis, 'at times is also one of contempt.'

She flushed, aware that he spoke the truth. She *had* revealed her contempt from time to time — by a glance or statement or even a casual comment. Yet always she seemed to hurt herself. It was as if she just had to get in a thrust now and then ... as a measure of self-defence against the growing conviction that he could affect her far more than would be comfortable for her peace of mind.

'And so you're thinking of retaliating?' was all she could find to say, since she was both embarrassed and unhappy. There was no denying it, each time she and Kane had words it was she who suffered most.

'You make no denial about the contempt, then?' he said, looking at her with an intentness that only increased her discomfiture. He was so superior, so much the master of the situation, that she felt inadequate and even subdued. Nevertheless, she rallied sufficiently to remind him that she had an excuse for her contempt. 'So we're back to Sandra again, are we?' Something most curious in his tone, and he was surely in a state of hesitancy? It was as if he were debating mentally, on something of great importance, endeavouring to come to a decision. 'Sandra, whom I let down so badly.'

'There was no excuse,' said Gail. 'Even if you didn't want to marry her you could have sent her money.'

He nodded, as he had before when this was mentioned.

'I could,' he said, again as before.

'If you keep Leta,' Gail pointed out, 'then at least you'd be making some sort of reparation. I'd – I'd admire you for that.'

'Thanks,' he returned acidly. 'But it may interest you to know that I'm not in the least troubled as to whether you admire me or not.'

She coloured painfully under the sarcasm and saw that Kane was deriving some considerable satisfaction from her discomfiture. But his countenance remained icily determined and she found herself saying,

'Would you really send Leta away?' Her tone pleaded, although she did not know it. She was troubled not only on Leta's account, but for some reason she was anxious for Kane too. She wanted him to succeed in his plan for his own sake as well as that of his daughter. She intensely disliked both Mrs. Farrell and her daughter; they were misfits in this stately home where harmony could have so easily prevailed – and most certainly had prevailed before Kane's father remarried. That he had chosen a woman like Rachel was incredible, and Kane himself must have said this time and time again.

'I shall certainly consider it if you continue to adopt this attitude.'

She said after some thought,

'I'm sorry. I'll try to remember who you are.'

He said nothing; he seemed to be interested in her expression and she did wonder if with his keen sense of perception he guessed that she was concerned for him as well as Leta. She spoke hesitantly, mentioning the fact that, while she and Leta remained, there was a chance that his plan would succeed, but that if they left he was back where he had started.

'Is the success of my plan of so much importance to you?' he inquired disconcertingly, and Gail swallowed before she spoke.

'Having met your stepmother I can understand your wanting her out of your house,' was her evasive reply, and it brought an unexpected glimmer of amusement to her companion's eyes. His whole appearance changed and she caught her breath involuntarily. Tension rose within her; her heart seemed to beat faster than it should, and once again she was admitting to the power of this man; owning that, when he changed like this, to a softened and faintly humorous mood, there was for her an appeal so strong that she became almost afraid.

'You avoid a direct answer, I see.' Kane spoke casually, but his gaze was keenly searching.

'I'm not so sure I understand you.' Again the evasion, and this time Kane dismissed the subject with a touch of impatience.

'It's of no matter.' A slight pause and then, with a glance towards the window, 'Send her to me later. I'll be in my room downstairs.'

Gail nodded her head.

'I must go down to breakfast,' she said after a little silence. 'It'll be getting cold, I left it to attend to Leta.'

'As I haven't had mine we'll have it together.'

Much later in the morning Rachel came to Gail when she was in the garden, relaxing with a book after having helped in the kitchen, clearing up and washing the enormous mountain of pots and dishes left by the hungry men.

'I want to talk to you.' Mrs. Farrell assumed a determined expression which quite naturally caused Gail a little unease. 'If I can have this other chair?'

'Of course.' Puzzled and on her guard, Gail asked if it was anything important.

'I'm having an hour with my book, as you can see,' she added. 'I hadn't expected to be disturbed.' This was the attitude which Kane had instructed her to take with his stepmother, and although Gail found such behaviour rather a strain, she accepted the inevitable, both to help Kane, and to hasten her own release from here.

'I must talk to you.' With a glowering look Rachel sat down on the garden chair, and turned towards Gail so that she looked straight into her face. 'There's something very strange about this whole situation,' she said. 'Something that doesn't fit.'

'Fit?' repeated Gail, assuming an air of bewilderment. 'I don't think I understand you?' Her voice was steady and calm, but how she wished that Kane would appear, as he had this morning, so unexpectedly, to save the situation. 'You'd better explain yourself.'

'That's exactly what I intend to do! You and that child appearing, out of the blue! Why haven't we heard of you before?'

Gail bristled and said again that the woman would have to explain what she meant.

'Is it my fault that Kane never mentioned his wife and child?' she went on, feeling that this would be the thing to say in these particular circumstances. 'It was natural for him to remain quiet about it, when the marriage had – at that time – broken up.'

'At what time?' Rachel's eyes were intently fixed

upon Gail's face. 'Kane's father used to talk to me for hours and hours, and yet he never so much as mentioned the fact that his son had taken a holiday in England. In fact,' continued Mrs. Farrell slowly, 'he told me that he had no relatives in England. I have no reason to believe that he would lie about such a thing, and therefore Kane couldn't have gone there to visit relatives, could he?' No answer from Gail who, despite her attempts at control, was suddenly aware of strange tinglings within her. Nerves quivered as she dwelt on what her companion had been saying. No relatives in England . . .

She frowned at last and said,

'I'm not willing, Mrs. Farrell, to discuss my husband, or his relatives in England—'

'Tell me,' interrupted Mrs. Farrell rudely, 'did you ever meet any of these relatives?' Again her eyes were watchfully intent. Gail turned away, hiding the fact that her colour had risen. This woman was indeed disconcerting, and involuntarily Gail's glance was directed towards the low line of hills where the dark silhouettes of men could be seen. Having dismounted, they were gathered in a group and Gail realized that they had stopped for smoke-oh. Sometimes Kane, if he were close enough to the homestead, would return for his morning break, going into the kitchen and finding himself something to eat. Would he return this morning? She found herself almost willing him to do so.

And like a miracle there he was!

'It's an answer to a prayer,' she gasped, but silently.

'Kane!' she called, for he was striding towards the verandah, not having glanced their way. Halting abruptly, he stood for a few seconds uncertainly and saw the swift frown that knit his brow. He was in a hurry, obviously, but she was not allowing him to leave her in this sort of position. 'Can you spare a few minutes?'

The frown deepened, but he came over to where she and his stepmother were sitting.

'What is it, dear?' he asked, smiling at his 'wife' affectionately. 'I'm in a hurry—'

'Rachel is asking questions which you're more competent to answer than I—' She rose as she spoke, the idea of total escape having come to her suddenly. 'So I'll leave you and get on with some jobs I have to catch up with.' Swiftly she was gone, having snatched up her book. Never a backward glance did she make, but she smiled faintly to herself because she could actually see the scowling expression on Rachel's face – and the arrogant one on Kane's.

He came to her less than five minutes later. She was in the sitting-room, a duster in her hand.

'What did you tell her?' Abrupt the question, examining the eyes. Was he troubled? she wondered. He appeared to be casual enough, but then he never did seem ruffled.

'Nothing at all. You arrived at a most opportune moment.' The relief in her voice could not escape him and she saw him smile, reassuringly. She responded, her mind flying to this morning and the breakfast they had taken together – their first meal alone. Kane had been different, more human. He it was who served her with bacon and eggs from the silver dish on the sideboard. It had a spirit lamp beneath it and so the food was piping hot. He it was who made fresh toast, using the electric toaster which was also on the sideboard. Revelling in this attention, Gail had herself been different. She was pleasant to him, as he was to her, and when it was over she found herself giving a small sigh of regret. 'She was asking me some awkward questions, though, and I felt that I'd find myself tied up in knots.'

He nodded sympathetically, rather to her surprise.

'I do realize just how awkward it all is for you, Gail.' This too surprised her and she wondered what had happened to the curt and impersonal manner which up till now had characterized his way with her – his way when they were alone, that was. In the presence of others he adopted a different manner altogether, bent as he was on giving the impression that he was in love with his 'wife'.

'She seemed convinced that you had no relatives in England.' A subtle inquiry to which he had an answer ready.

'She and I have been over this before. She knows full well that I have relatives in England. It was said merely to draw you out. She's suspicious, which is only natural, but she hasn't anything concrete on which to base those suspicions.'

'She said that your father talked to her a great deal, and yet he had never mentioned your trip to England.'

'She lies when she says Father talked to her a great deal. He was a preoccupied kind of man, talking little to anyone, even to me. Moreover, he didn't happen to get along with our relations and consequently never mentioned them, not to anyone other than me, that is. And even then it was unusual for him to do so.'

Gail hesitated, and Kane talked a little more, just to reassure her, and he succeeded.

'I see now what you mean about her methods of drawing me out,' she said thoughtfully when he had finished speaking. 'I shall be on my guard in future.'

'Try to avoid being alone with her,' he advised, and then, changing the subject, 'We'll be preparing for your party quite soon. This evening you can come along to my sitting-room and we'll discuss it.'

She coloured enchantingly.

'It's good of you to bother, Kane.' She was shy all at once and wondered if he were amused at this, because he did seem to curve his lips in the glimmer of a smile.

'Not at all. It's necessary. We always use birthdays and the like as excuses for having a party. It would look most odd indeed were I not to give a party for your birthday.'

'You needn't have mentioned my birthday to anyone.' She looked wryly at him. 'It isn't as if I'm to be here for more than a few months, is it?'

His eyes revealed nothing as he replied,

'That's something of which we can't be sure.'

She frowned up at him, aware of a constriction of nerves.

'My parents won't expect me to be gone for very long.'

His stare was lingering.

'You're tired of our way of life – already?'

'Not at all; I love it here.' Her reply was spontaneous and sincere. Kane's straight brows lifted a fraction.

'You surprise me. Most English girls soon tire of our silence, our loneliness.'

'You have many English girls here?' Gail knew that some girls came into the Never-Never for adventure, obtaining posts as home helps on these cattle stations.

'They come and go.' Kane's glance strayed to the window and, following its direction, Gail saw the small flock of lovely rosellas, their red, blue and yellow feathers dazzlingly emphasized by the sunlight. Kane seemed lost in thought, as he teetered back on his heels, his hands half in and half out of the pockets of his tight-fitting jeans. 'They're full of enthusiasm on arrival. Oh, yes, they can stand the loneliness – it's what they've always wanted, to get away from it all. Sometimes they stick it out until the end of their term, but in the main they break, declaring this to be a wilderness, a no-man's-land. They crave for lights and cafés and shops, for the scurry of the bus or train before the tea and television session.' Contempt now in his low and languid tone. He shook his head to illustrate his scorn. 'Why do they come, I wonder?'

An uneasy silence followed, with Gail half wishing he would go, and yet aware that there would be a tiny void as soon as he had done so.

'You've had them here, at Vernay Downs, then?' She spoke a little breathlessly, urged to break the silence because it seemed like a weight on the atmosphere.

'We've had them here, yes,' was his non-committal reply, and after another silence Gail spoke again.

'If I had come as a home help, I am sure I'd have stayed at least until the end of my term.' Her eyes wandered to the window again. The MacDonnell Ranges seemed close in the brilliant white light of the sun. In the foreground a billabong shone brightly, its edges frilled with casuarina trees, while to the east lay the river from which the billabong had been cut off, but the bed was dry and bounder-strewn; it meandered close to the homestead and the eucalypts growing along its banks provided shade for anyone wanting to take a walk or a ride on horseback. Leta, who was often seen riding with Dave, went this way with him, and once or twice Gail had walked along the dry creek bed to meet them on their way back to the paddock.

'I half believe you would.' Kane's response came at length, and he looked down into her face, an odd expression on his own. Gail smiled, conscious, as always, of his attractions. That particular expression which softened the slate-grey eyes, that prominent chin and firm lean jawline, the dark skin, the clearly-chiselled lines that spelled pride and clearly marked him as one of the aristocrats of the Outback. 'I must be off,' he said at last, but, strangely, no action followed his words.

'And I must finish my dusting.' She felt awkward, as she so often did when in his presence. This morning at breakfast had been an exception, as was part of this present little interlude. But now there was a tenseness in the room; she was more than a little affected by it and with a jerky, nervous gesture she began making the duster into a small pad. 'A little help from me makes it easier for the lubras,' she added lamely when Kane did not speak. Why had he come back to the house? If it was for the customary reason of wanting something to eat then why didn't he leave her, and make for the kitchen? It was so unlike him to remain with her like this, for no apparent reason at all.

He looked down at her, faintly smiling.

'You appear to enjoy working,' he said.

'I'd rather be doing something than be idle all the time.'

'Most commendable.'

'Not at all; I'm keeping myself from being bored.'

His eyes flickered; they slid down from her face to her neck, then to her tiny waist and lastly to her legs and ankles. A soft blush fused her cheeks; she moved nervously, then forced a smile to her lips. She saw his mouth relax, his eyes take on a softened expression. He seemed unable to bring his eyes from her and she turned at length and began dusting an antique occasional table.

'Don't forget what I said about coming to my room this evening after dinner,' he said and, with a lift of a hand in salute, he strode from the room.

CHAPTER EIGHT

THE evening was cool and fresh after the searing heat of the afternoon and Gail was reluctant to leave her most comfortable place on the verandah. She had come out immediately after dinner, intending to enjoy the breeze for a few minutes before going to Kane's room. Dave had asked her to walk with him, but she had explained, in low tones as she sat next to him at the table, that they must be careful on account of the vindictiveness of Mrs. Farrell and Ertha. She told him what had happened on the occasion when they went out into the bush; he had scowled and thrown Mrs. Farrell a darkling glance. This was seen by Kane, who instantly raised his eyebrows and flashed a glance at Gail.

'Don't talk about it,' urged Gail to Dave. 'Kane's seen you glaring at his stepmother.'

'What a pickle!' he exclaimed exasperatedly, but in response to her plea he had changed the subject to something trivial, something that had not to be discussed in undertones.

But now he came out to her and she looked up with a smile.

'I thought you'd be going over to your friend's,' she said, but glanced at the chair opposite to her.

'Jim, you mean?' He shook his head as he sat down.

'He's off on a fortnight's holiday tomorrow, so he won't want me around now.' Automatically Dave's eyes wandered to the small bungalow which stood all on its own in a lush, flower-filled garden. Only the lights could be discerned from here, but these were on in every room and Dave smiled faintly as she added,

'They'll be busy packing. Betty's so excited at the idea of bringing back their daughter.'

Gail looked interested.

'I didn't know they had a daughter. You've spoken of Jim and Betty once or twice, saying what good friends they've been to you, but you never mentioned a daughter.'

'I suppose,' replied Dave thoughtfully, 'it's because I've never seen her.'

'She's married?'

Dave shook his head.

'No, she works in Perth. They all lived there until two years ago, but then Jim decided he wanted an outdoor job and he and Betty moved out here, Jim having got the job of stockrider. He was a stockrider in his youth and left the Outback when he met Betty while he was on holiday in Perth. She didn't want to leave her family, so they bought a house and settled down. Georgina – that's the daughter – had a splendid job, so she didn't want to come with them. In any case, there's nothing here for a girl of eighteen.'

'She's only eighteen?'

'She was then. She's twenty now.'

'She's coming for a holiday only?'

'I have an idea they're going to try to persuade her to stay permanently. She's been teaching in a private school which has closed down and as the Boss will soon be short of a teacher Georgina could fit in nicely.'

Gail nodded, aware that one of the teachers was leaving next month. She was marrying a grazier from a station two hundred miles away, a man she had met at one of Kane's shed dances a few months previously.

'It would be nice for your friends; they sound homely, the sort who like to have their children with them if possible.' She drifted off into a pensive silence and Dave asked her curiously,

'Are you dreaming of home, and your parents?' He seemed faintly disconsolate as the question was asked and Gail looked up with a friendly smile.

'Yes, Dave, I was.'

'You're looking forward to going back?'

She nodded, but not with any enthusiasm.

'I love it here, but my parents wouldn't be happy for me to stay, even if that were possible.'

He made no comment and for a long moment there was silence between them.

'It's a bit of a muddle, isn't it?' he said at last. 'I said I'd like to get to know you better, and I meant it.'

She swallowed hard.

'Dave, I don't think we ought to talk about such things.'

He looked at her through shrewd and frank brown eyes.

'You like me, just a little, don't you, Gail?' The question was out and she coloured delicately. Somehow she had known that it was bound to come some time. And she had to answer truthfully and the answer was yes. He nodded his head as if he had never doubted what her answer would be. 'What are we going to do, then?' He was brisk all at once, and she frowned as the great difficulties crowded in upon her.

'It's better that we don't talk about it,' she said again. 'I'm Kane's wife as far as everyone is concerned—'

'Everyone?' he cut in swiftly.

'Kane's giving a party for my birthday and all his friends will be here. I wonder if Kane took an assessment of all the difficulties that must result from this deception.'

'He'll have something ready. I believe in your supposition that he'll just spread it about that you became fed up with our way of life and deserted him again.'

138

'It seems the only way that I can visualize.'

'But us . . .?' Brief the query and Gail had no answer to it. 'There must be some way in which we can get together – eventually, I mean.' Another pause while he waited once again for her to speak. She shrugged her shoulders and glanced at her watch. It was time she was going to see Kane, but she had not the heart to terminate this interlude and send Dave away to spend the time brooding, on his own somewhere in the garden or upstairs in his room. 'I could follow you to England,' he suggested, but now it seemed to Gail that he was moving far too fast for her.

'I don't know if I want that,' she had to say. 'After all, we've not really had a chance to get to know one another, let alone . . .' She trailed off, her colour rising again. Dave's forehead creased in a frown.

'We *must* find an opportunity of seeing one another – just occasionally.'

'We see one another several times each day,' she reminded him.

'You know what I mean, Gail,' he returned almost angrily. 'I mean – alone!'

'It would be far too risky. Kane would be furious if scandal and gossip resulted from anything I did.'

'I can understand that,' he replied with a little less heat. 'All the same, you're not married, and therefore he should realize that you're free to do as you wish.'

'I'm free, yes, but I've made him a promise to pose as his wife. I must keep that promise, Dave; I must – it wouldn't say much for my integrity were I to let him down.'

He had to agree, but she saw that he was thinking hard, endeavouring to find a way out of the difficulties. 'Dave,' she said at length, taking another glance at her watch, 'I have to see Kane about my party. He says there are things to discuss—' She looked apologetically at him, 'I'm sorry . . .'

He smiled to put her mind at ease and she thought again what a nice person he was.

'All right, Gail.' He paused and his eyes wandered. 'You've noticed how the colour of the MacDonnell Ranges changes according to the time of the day?' he said, diverted. She looked first at him and then at the dark outline of the mountains. He was in a sort of brooding mood and she recalled her own conclusion that he was a lonely man.

'Yes, I've noticed. They're flame at dawn and change throughout the day until, at night, they are a deep purple like this.' She allowed her eyes to travel along the summits. 'They're far more beautiful when the moon is out.'

He nodded absently, and then looked at her.

'I must let you go,' he said, and they both got up from their chairs. 'Good night, Gail.'

'Good night.'

He followed her into the room, then stopped. 'Tell Leta I'll be free tomorrow at four o'clock. We'll go riding.'

Gail nodded and promised to mention this to Leta.

'She loves riding with you,' she murmured, and again he nodded his head.

'I could make something of her.' His lips went tight and suddenly Gail's heart contracted. She said impulsively,

'Dave, how is it that you haven't married before now?'

He turned his head to look full into her face.

'How often does a man meet girls in a place like this?' he asked.

'But you have holidays.'

He seemed to laugh within himself — a short and humourless laugh.

'A couple of weeks now and then. What am I supposed to do – rush around taking a look at any girl who happens to cross my path, eyeing her with a view to making a snap decision and asking her to marry me?'

Although frowning heavily at his sarcasm, Gail allowed it to pass, understanding and compassion rising within her.

'It's difficult, I can see that.' She forced a smile to her lips as she added, 'At my party – you might meet someone there . . .' And then she trailed off, aware of her lack of tact.

'I don't happen to want to meet anyone now,' he told her seriously. 'I want – somehow – to find a solution to this problem of our not being able to see one another alone. You've admitted that you like me and that's a beginning. We'll find a way,' he ended, and before she could make any comment he had said good night again and turned back on to the verandah.

She was looking troubled when she entered her 'husband's' room and she saw his eyes narrow slightly. He was sitting comfortably in a deep armchair but rose on her entry.

'Sit down, Gail.' He drew a chair forward and she took possession of it. He was obviously in a mellow mood and she did wish she could have opened up and told him what was on her mind.

'No,' she lied, 'it's only that I'm feeling rather tired.'

'You are? You'd rather leave this until tomorrow evening?'

She shook her head at this.

'I'm not too tired to do what's necessary.'

'There isn't anything to do, exactly,' he smiled, sitting down again. 'But naturally we must talk about your party. You'll be wanting to know what kind of people are coming. You will also have to be briefed, of

141

course.' He was expressing faint amusement and she found herself smiling in response even though she murmured something about being scared. 'Nonsense,' he said, passing that off on the instant. 'Why should you feel scared? You have me there for support.'

'Meeting so many strangers . . . and also, I'm going to feel strange because we're supposed to have been separated. Everyone will believe that it was all my fault.'

The slate-grey eyes opened very wide.

'Why on earth should they believe that?'

'Well . . . They're going to think that I wouldn't face the life out here.' The window behind him was wide open and she allowed her eyes to travel to the dark void that was the plain. 'What else can they think?'

Kane answered quietly,

'I've already been in touch with everyone who matters – over the air, of course. I've explained that it was all my fault—'

'Did they believe you?' The question was out before she realized just what had prompted it. Kane seemed far too honourable a man to marry and then decide it was all a mistake. And yet . . . he was *not* an honourable man; this had been proved.

'Why should they disbelieve me?' he asked her curiously, and, when she offered no reply, 'I'm a cad, remember – the type to make a mistake like that and then with a shrug of my shoulders forget all about it.'

Gail lost a little of her colour. And that odd little access of doubt rose up again. She was suddenly floundering in uncertainty, like someone lost and not knowing which way to turn.

'I did say, if you remember, that I couldn't believe you were the cad we had all branded you.' Not in the least diplomatic, but she had to speak plainly to him.

His eyes kindled for a space, but then they portrayed

142

a sort of amused satire as he returned, his voice low and carrying a faintly husky note which always sounded so attractive to Gail,

'But what about Leta? Isn't she proof that I'm the cad you branded me?'

She looked down at her hands, strangely reluctant to agree with what he had said. She tried to analyse her emotions, tried to tell herself that she should retain her contempt for this man ... Mechanically she shook her head, her thoughts going for a moment to Sandra. Could there possibly have been some blame on her part?

Suddenly Gail found herself saying, as she looked across at Kane, looked into steadfast grey eyes that never flinched under her stare,

'You told me to remember that there are always parts unknown.' Her voice was low, and not quite clear, for in her throat was a constriction that made speech most difficult. 'You – you didn't explain, though?' A question – and a plea. Gail now knew for sure that she wished for nothing more than to be told that Kane had not been entirely to blame for what had happened.

His eyes were soft; her voice contained a gentle note, a note that held a wealth of understanding.

'I can't explain, my dear. But just you keep on remembering about those parts unknown.' He looked kindly at her and said, 'It's all puzzling to you; I can see this. But be patient, Gail, and do the job you promised to do. It doesn't really matter whether or not you understand everything, since when your job is done you'll be leaving here and never returning.'

She moved her tongue, swallowing the moisture that had collected on it. '. . . you'll be leaving here and never returning.' Unemotional tones, even though the kindly expression remained. Gail was acutely conscious of a dead weight within her, of a sort of hopelessness which she could not even begin to explain.

'Kane,' she said at last, and her eyes were far too bright as they looked into his, 'I wish you would explain – just a little?'

He shook his head and once again he was the Boss of Vernay Downs, authoritative, inflexible.

'It's quite unnecessary. You're here to do this job; you are in fact an employee—' His eyebrows lifted in a gesture of inquiry. 'You will agree about that, I think?'

She nodded and said yes, she did agree.

'But—'

'No arguments,' he interrupted on a note of finality that gave its own warning. 'As you're an employee of mine it's not either necessary or desirable that you should be given any details about my personal affairs. If you'll keep that in mind, Gail, then it will save any unpleasantness between us.'

She flushed uncomfortably and turned her face away from him. Her voice quivered as she said,

'I shall make sure to keep it in mind, Kane.'

'Good!' He then changed the subject and they discussed details of the party. She would not be pestered with questions, this he promised her, and although she would not venture to inquire how he knew, she was extremely puzzled, simply because it would only be natural for people to ply her with questions. However, she would have to wait and see what happened. She was given a picture of the activities and despite her anxiety she could not help but be a little excited at the prospect of so expensive and well-organized a party being given for her – even though it was only for appearances' sake, a mere business event that was, in her 'husband's' opinion, necessary.

The day arrived and still the preparations continued, preparations which had been going on for several days. The party was to be in the large barn which stood some distance from the house. Its name was rather deceiving since it was beautifully constructed of pine with polished blood-wood floor and panelled walls. Concealed lights ran all round the ceiling, which was raftered and festooned with brightly-coloured paper flowers and streamers. Outside was a surrounding garden complete with massive lawn – on which sprinklers worked regularly – flower borders and of course trees of many varieties. Secluded arbours abounded, and a lovely ornamental pool also had seats set around it, partially hidden by the bushes growing close to its edges. In the centre of the pool was a waterfall and a beautiful piece of statuary – a group of cherubs – from which came several coloured lights – pink, deep rose and yellow. Part of the pool was covered with mauve lilies, and black and white ducks swam about among them.

'All this is for you, Mummy,' cried Leta as she and Gail watched the three lubras setting out the long table with pretty cloths, prior to the important event of bringing out the food. 'Will I be having a party like this?'

'Of course – when it's your birthday.'

'I'll have all my friends from school, won't I?'

Gail looked down at her.

'Have you made some more friends, then?'

Leta's eyes shone.

'Yes, they all like me – not hitting me as they did when I went to the other school!'

'But you hit them first, remember.'

'Only because they didn't like me!'

Was it all a vicious circle? Gail was asking herself when on looking round she saw Dave coming across the ochre-coloured ground that separated the barn and its gardens from the home paddock.

'Hello there, you two!' he was greeting them a moment later as he slid from his horse. He was hot and dusty, but there was a brightness in his eyes as they settled on Leta. Playfully he ruffled her hair and she laughed up at him. Gail's eyes flickered as she watched; this was a strange relationship which had sprung up between Dave and Leta. In fact, she was sure that the relationship was stronger and closer than that between Leta and her father. Come to think of it, Kane showed practically no interest at all in his daughter. He accepted her and yet she was just left to get along — another addition to the household as it were, but one of no real importance, of no importance other than that of making herself a nuisance to Mrs. Farrell, that was. 'What have you been doing, my little one — other than giving cheek to certain people, that is?'

A grin of pure mischief looked out from those vivid blue eyes, eyes that were not unlike Dave's when it came to expressiveness.

'Being good!' she chuckled, and again he tousled her hair. Fascinated by the way they were with each other, Gail stood aside, content to be the silent onlooker. Never had anyone ruffled Leta's hair and got away without a kick in the shins or a finger being viciously bitten.

'Fibber! The truth — or we don't go riding—'

'Ooh . . . Are we going riding? I want Sinner; he's not so quiet as Sunstorm—'

'Not so fast!' he interrupted sternly. 'I asked what you had been doing?'

'Reading my book — truly!'

'Has she?' he asked Gail.

'Yes, as a matter of fact she's been sitting quietly with a book. I couldn't make out what had got into her. I didn't ask, as you can imagine — not when she was quiet like that! I left her alone.'

Dave gave a laugh and returned his attention to Leta.

'Very well, so long as you've done as you were told you shall have Sinner.'

'Oh, but—' Gail looked at him in some consternation, 'I heard Kane say that Sinner was far too frisky even for an experienced child . . .'

'I'm riding Sinner!' stamped Leta, glaring up at her. 'You mind your own business! Dave knows what I want. He knows I'm a good rider!'

'Will it be all right?' Gail asked, and he nodded at once, reassuringly.

'She's cut out for something more challenging than Sunstorm. Yes, she'll be all right. I'll be alongside her, so you've no need to worry.'

Gail relaxed, confident that Dave would know what he was doing. And he did. A couple of hours later Gail happened to be by the paddock when the two came riding back after having ridden their horses hard, judging by the sweat on the animals' necks.

'She's going to be a champion! I'm entering her in the gymkhana!'

Gail frowned. *I'm* entering her . . .

'Will that be all right with Kane?' she felt bound to ask.

'I shouldn't think he'll mind.'

'I want to ride in the gymkhana! I want to beat everybody else!'

'And you will!' declared Dave. How happy he looked, thought Gail, wondering if he had resigned himself to the fact that he and she herself could never be more than the casual acquaintances which they were at the present time. But she discovered differently later in the evening when, looking inordinately attractive in a lightweight jacket and fine worsted

147

trousers, he invited her to dance.

'You look adorable!' he exclaimed as he drew her into his arms. 'Gail, I'm beginning to fall in love with you!'

'No, Dave, it mustn't happen!'

'Why not?' He held her from him and looked questioningly at her. 'We'll think of something when the time of your freedom comes along, you'll see.'

'If we did get together in that way, then you couldn't stay here.'

'That's for sure. But I can settle anywhere where you want to settle.'

'I don't believe that, Dave,' she returned with a wise little smile. 'This is the life you've been accustomed to and it's the life you love.'

He made no reply and for the rest of the dance they were silent. When at length he took her back to the table where she had a drink half finished, he shook his head a little dejectedly and said,

'Why did you come, Gail, upsetting my life like this?' But she had no time to answer, for at that moment Kane arrived at the table and silently invited her to dance. Slipping into his outstretched arms, she found herself being whirled away, floating as if on air as Kane's long legs found a way between the dancers to the edge of the floor where there was not only more room but where they could enjoy the breeze drifting in from the open windows.

'You seem rather fond of Dave.' Quiet the tone and yet there was a strange undercurrent about it. 'And he of you.'

'That's true,' she replied, seeing no harm in this small admission.

'And yet he knows you're married to me?' Suspicion in the voice? She rather thought so, but she merely gave the careless reply,

'We like each other as friends. Isn't that permissible?'

'Of course. But remember, Gail, you're not to run any risks.' A pause as he afforded her time to speak, but as he saw that she was not accepting the opportunity he went on, 'I don't expect, though, that Dave will go beyond what is correct behaviour; he's always afforded me the respect which is due to me.' He was speaking in tones little above a whisper and she realized it was to himself rather than to her.

'You're sure of Dave, but not of me?' She could not resist this challenge and she saw him give a small start as it struck him just what he had said.

'My apologies,' he returned, surprising her. 'I should know by now that you're to be trusted.'

'Thank you.' She was shy all at once, and felt very small in his arms. And she felt safe, too, just as if she really were his wife. 'I must thank you for this wonderful party, too. You've been so generous—'

'Forget it,' he broke in curtly. 'You know very well that it was a necessity.'

'But you had no need to go to such great expense, surely?'

'We always do this sort of thing in a big way, as you'll see when we attend Craig Bowden's party next month.'

'We're going to a party?'

'He's giving it for his son's birthday. Yes, of course we shall be going.' They were dancing in perfect harmony and Gail thought she had never before enjoyed a dance so much. For one thing, many girls were turning their heads to stare at them with eyes that would invariably come to rest with envy on Gail's flushed face. And she had actually overheard one pretty girl saying, to another of about Gail's own age,

'The lucky thing! And just to think, Kane was married all the time! I'd never let him go off and leave me if I were married to him. She must have been out of her mind!'

'Are you warm?' Kane asked the question and all unthinking she replied,

'I'm more than warm, I'm hot! I could do with a breath of fresh air.'

'So could I,' he returned promptly, and before she knew she was being steered with the deftest of manoeuvres towards the french window. Once through it Kane released her and she fell into step beside him as he made for one of the tables set in romantic seclusion under the spreading foliage of a clump of ghost gums.

'You would like something to eat?' he queried, but she shook her head.

'I'm not hungry at the moment – but, if you are . . .?'

'No, I don't want anything just now.' He leant back in his chair, hitched up the leg of his trousers and, crossing one leg over the other, stared at her from this most relaxed position on the opposite side of the table. 'You're enjoying yourself?'

She answered spontaneously, her eyes bright and very revealing.

'This is a night I shall always remember!'

A smiled curved the firm hard mouth.

'It's come up to your expectations, apparently.'

'It's exceeded them. Oh, Kane, that food! How do the lubras do it? They're expert enough to make a trade of it.'

'They're clever, undoubtedly, although it's Daisybell mainly.' He paused a moment and then, 'You haven't been plied with questions, that's quite plain.'

'Because I would soon have mentioned it to you?' she asked with a wry quiver of her lips. 'I certainly would have done !'

'But I did assure you that no one would be asking questions – at least the kind of questions which might cause you embarrassment.'

'I was asked how I'm liking it here now. And once I was asked if I would be able to settle.'

His lips curved again.

'And your answer?' he queried, his eyes subjecting her to a close scrutiny.

'I said yes, I was determined to settle. It was a little embarrassing now and then, though. For example, when Mr. Dryden asked the date of our marriage. He seemed to think that you hadn't been in England at the time that I said – when I answered him, that was.'

Kane frowned suddenly. Was he alert all at once? Impossible to read the mask which had come over his handsome countenance, and she gave up the attempt, admitting that it was futile anyway.

'What date did you give him?'

Gail told him and he seemed to frown more heavily.

'Was I wrong?' she questioned, troubled. 'I calculated and decided that the best date to give was nine months before Leta was born because, when you give a birthday party for her, people might just begin to calculate.' This appeared to amuse him, because his frown faded and his grey eyes took on a rather humorous light.

'I shouldn't think the men would, but the women might. Women seem to be made that way.'

Gail looked at him, uncertain as to whether or not she had heard a hint of contempt in his voice as he uttered that last sentence.

'Did I do right?' she wanted to know. 'I was so confused, not having expected a question like that.'

'You did very well, from what I can see.' He fell into

a thoughtful silence before he said, quite coolly and in his customary slow Australian drawl, 'It's only to be expected that people are amazed – or were, when first I told them that my wife and child had arrived here. But they'll get over it all in no time. Just another nine days' wonder. We have them sometimes out here in the bush.'

Gail said nothing, but she did try to picture the manner in which this cool collected man had put the news over to them all. He had certainly made a success of it, for apart from the few curious ones who had put the odd question to her, there had been interest only in her appearance and several times Kane had been congratulated on his 'wife's' beauty. No one, however, had ventured to voice the words which, to Gail, were the obvious ones to voice, words that conveyed surprise that he could have married her and then left her in England while he himself returned to his own country, and to his estate here in the Outback.

Leta was also accepted without much comment. She had been allowed to attend the party and stay for an hour and a half providing only that she behaved.

'One small sign of a tantrum and you'll be carried back to the house and be put to bed,' her father had threatened. And he had added that, although she must not answer any questions that might be put to her, she must not tell anyone to mind his or her own business. Leta had been on her best behaviour, spending some of her time with Kane and some with Dave. And in the end it was Dave who had taken her back to the homestead, carrying her on his shoulder, while Gail, a most odd expression in her eyes, had stood and watched Kane, totally unconcerned, chattering with some of his friends, cattle graziers from stations so far away that they were staying the night at Vernay Downs.

CHAPTER NINE

NEITHER Mrs. Farrell nor her daughter had put in an appearance at the party and it was only natural that their absence should be noticed, and commented upon. Kane replied non-committally to the questions asked, and as she noted the way in which his words were received Gail understood a little better how he had come to be able to escape questioning where she herself was concerned. Kane's friends and acquaintances knew that he would not tolerate any curiosity where his private affairs were concerned. Gossip there might be, but among themselves, and with no attempt to draw out the man concerned. Her admiration for Kane increased with this knowledge of his total withdrawal, and authoritative manner of conducting his affairs.

He himself remarked on the absence of the two women when next he danced with Gail.

'They were invited,' he told her indifferently. 'It was up to them whether or not they accepted the invitation.'

'I can't really blame them for not coming. They dislike me intensely – which is only natural, of course.'

He glanced down at her, his clear-cut features dark and austere in the dim lighting of the wide verandah on which they were dancing. Kane had come out because once again he was feeling the heat, as was Gail herself. The night was rather too warm, in fact, and even out here there was very little breeze.

'You've survived their malice much better than I expected,' was Kane's statement as he swung her right to the end of the verandah, where the steps were situated.

'It hasn't been easy — as of course, you warned me it wouldn't be.'

'Nevertheless, you've done very well indeed. I have an idea that they won't be with us for much longer.'

'You have?' In her surprise she leaned away from him, staring up into his eyes. 'Has something happened to bring about this optimism?'

'Nothing concrete,' he admitted, but went on to say that he had seen Rachel going through the large bookcase in the hall, and taking out those books which were hers.

'Does that really mean anything, Kane?'

'She's also removed some small ornaments from one or two rooms — ornaments which she brought with her.'

'I see . . .' Gail felt a sudden sinking of her heart. 'So I might be going from here sooner than we expected?'

No answer, strangely. Kane changed the subject altogether, asking if she had noticed that Dave was dancing most of the time with Georgina, who had arrived only that very evening and in consequence she and her parents had put in an appearance only about an hour and a half ago.

'No, I hadn't noticed,' she had to admit. The truth was that she was revelling in being with Kane who, for effect, was as attentive as any loving husband could be. He had brought her the food and the wine; he had danced with her for more than half the time, and he had taken her out on two occasions for a breath of fresh air. And now they were out again, but this time he was intending to take a stroll, for he asked her if she required a wrap. 'No,' she answered, 'I'm still very warm.'

He took her hand, much to her surprise, for there was no one to see them now, and they went down the steps and walked out into the night.

'This is better.' He referred to the cooler atmosphere, she surmised ... or could it possibly be that he had wanted to get away from the crowd, and come out into the peace and quietness of the garden? Memory brought incidents crowding into her mind, incidents that had occurred during the past fortnight, ever since that evening when he had had her in his room and talked to her about the forthcoming party. He had been so different, so kind and so tolerant. There had not been any dissension between them as there had been before; no arguments over Leta, no icy rebukes from Kane, no indignant comments from Gail herself. In fact, a pleasant sort of relationship had developed, a harmony that resulted in Gail's almost forgetting that Kane had ever been so callous as to let her cousin down. For now she was becoming overwhelmed with doubts, and one of those doubts was that there could be some feasible explanation for his conduct at that particular time; this was strengthened every time his gravely-spoken words entered her mind, words about 'parts unknown'.

He retained her hand in his and she wondered whether he himself was aware of this, for he had become pensive, preoccupied, as he walked across the lawn towards the clump of trees under which seats were partially screened from the view of anyone coming out on to the verandah of the shed. Gail, her heart beating far too quickly, because of the fact that he had her hand in his, and because the night held magic – the music and dancing and the gay but muted lights – walked beside him, profoundly aware of him as a man, conscious as never before of his superlative attractions. Her eyes wandered, out into the infinity of the bush, this stronghold of rugged pastoralists whose domains were measured in square miles, not acres.

155

She mused on conversations she had heard among these graziers; she had learned that all of them owned vast estates which, like that of Kane, were self-contained communities with their own airfields, villages, shops and schools. Doctors, nurses, hospitals which could deal with all but the serious cases . . . everything was there, in this wild and weathered country, this 'centre', as it was termed by the Australians whose home it was.

'Are you all right?' Soft the tone and faintly anxious as Kane glanced down at her. She nodded, finding difficulty in voicing anything while she was wrapped in the magic of the night like this. Kane smiled, one of his rare and most attractive smiles; her lashes fluttered as shyness overcame her and Kane laughed then and his hand tightened around hers. In her heart something leapt and she turned her head from his disconcerting gaze, returning her attention to the bush again. There was something ruthless about it of which she was potentially aware at this particular time, yet it excited her and she felt a strange constriction in her throat.

They reached the trees and Kane stopped, for some reason hesitating before he invited her to sit down. Several seats were occupied and as Gail noted this she suddenly wanted to get away, into the solitude out there, into the moonlit wilds. The longing for isolation from everyone around her – everyone except Kane, that was – became an urgent necessity as she stood there, faintly aloof, her beautiful face and figure revealed in the silver glow of the moonlight that spread over the bush.

'What is it . . .?' The question was almost a caress, and so affected was she that she feared the wild throbbing of her heart would suffocate her. And if it didn't, then surely this constriction in her throat would choke her. 'Gail,' he murmured, 'you're very beautiful.'

She blushed adorably but, still shy and unsure of herself, could offer no more than a simple 'thank you' in return.

'Would you care to walk?' he asked, just as if he knew how she was feeling.

'I'd love to walk.'

'Come, then,' and he tugged gently until she fell into step beside him. The garden was soon left behind as they turned towards the hazy blue hills above which were deep pools of shade created by the long dark shadows sent forth from the impressive backcloth of the MacDonnell Mountains.

'How wonderful it all is!' The words were whispered as Gail looked up at the man beside her, her eyes bright in the light of the full moon. 'Look, Kane, at the beautiful Southern Cross!'

He smiled faintly, but refrained from reminding her that the sight was not entirely new to him. She knew what she had said, though, and a self-deprecating laugh left her lips.

Once the lights were left behind Kane slowed down his pace, and they walked very slowly – like lovers, she thought, not daring to move her fingers lest he would release her hand. She made a determined effort to be calm, but it was not easy when her heart was beating over-rate like this. A sort of exquisite fear had taken possession of her; she knew a recklessness one moment, but the next moment there was the picture of Sandra, the sweet-natured girl who had died because of this man, because he had allowed her to fall in love with him when he knew full well that he intended leaving her when, his holiday in England having come to an end, he would return to his home here, in the Outback.

'Parts unknown ...' A warning creeping into her mind, intruding into all these other reflections, a warning strong as the man who had spoken it . . .

'Kane,' she exclaimed, the words tumbling from her lips before she could stop them, 'tell me something about your visit to England—' But she stopped, having got that far, and put a nervous finger to her mouth.

Kane turned his head, and looked down at her, his eyes flickering with an odd expression, an expression she had seen once before — when he appeared to be caught in a web of indecision. She had gained the impression then that he was debating whether or not to disclose something, and she had the same impression now. But to her utter disappointment he shook his head.

'You wouldn't be interested, Gail.' Although his tone was gentle enough there was a familiar firmness about it which warned Gail not to ask any more questions on that particular subject.

'I'm sorry,' she said, and the disappointment was clearly ringing in her voice. 'I should mind my own business.'

For the next few minutes there was silence between them, a not very pleasant silence, and Gail was angry with herself for allowing her curiosity to come to the surface. However, as they continued along the gibber path which for some reason Kane had taken, a conversation took place between them and soon Gail was finding magic in the night again.

Kane was telling her about life on the station and she listened with keen interest, inserting a question now and then; he appeared pleased that she should want to know more and he would answer these questions fully and with patience.

'I was so surprised by the fact that the community is self-supporting,' she told him. 'I knew of course that your estate was very large, but somehow I pictured a lonely house with a few buildings around it — barns and stables and the like—'

'Just as your farmers in England have?' he broke in with some amusement. 'Well, Gail, that wouldn't be much use here, would it?'

'No, indeed it wouldn't. You have many other villages – scattered about the estate?'

'But of course. This estate, and many like it, are, as you know, as large as counties. Villages are a necessity, the grazing being so scattered as it is.'

'It's all so vast that it takes time to assimilate all the facts. Tell me some more, Kane.'

'About the life, or the business of rearing cattle?'

'Both.'

He smiled then, his amusement returning. Her heart seemed to jerk right into her throat, because of the attractiveness of him and because – despite his refusal to answer her question about his visit to England – she felt that no disunity whatsoever had come between them this evening. She felt close to him for the first time, his equal, his friend ... Friend? Gail knew the question hovered at the back of her subconscious, but she erected a barrier between it and her more foremost thoughts. It was a question she must continue to bar ...

Kane began to speak, telling her about the work of mustering the cattle, of the work done in the branding yards, of the eventual dispatching of the 'fats' to the great centres of Darwin and Brisbane, where they would be killed for meat.

'You send them by train, and air, don't you? I've read that they used to be sent with drovers. What a journey that must have been!'

'Yes, indeed,' he agreed musingly, and went on to tell her that graves could be found all along the roads of the Outback, graves of men who had died while doing their duty. 'The most disastrous of droving trips was when five drovers, all white men, were taking over one and a half thousand cattle from Wollogorang to a station in the north – Arafura Station. The journey got one man down completely and he shot himself. Another wandered off into the bush and another deserted. A man named Dunbar died of fever near Roper's Bar and his grave is there still.' Kane paused, a heavy frown creasing his forehead, and Gail asked him what had happened to the fifth man. 'He went on, even though the fever had got him too—'

'Oh, how awful! Imagine one poor man dragging himself on and on, and with the fever too!'

'His grave is by a lagoon—'

'He died? Oh, I had hoped he would have got through.'

Kane shook his head, looking at her with a curious light in his slate-grey eyes.

'A lubra living wild brought him water, and lily roots, but he died, despite her care.'

Gail frowned in silence, feeling so sad that she could almost have cried.

'Those poor men ... The one who went into the bush ...?'

'He would surely die. The bush is a killer, and that's why I was so stern in my warning when you first came, remember?' Gail did, since the warning had in fact been a definite order, with a threat of punishment should she disobey it. 'You will answer to me if I hear of your venturing into the bush alone,' he had said.

'The cattle, Kane. Would they all go wild, as your bulls sometimes do?'

Kane shook his head. He and Gail had reached the billabong and he stopped under the trees.

'The blacks from Arnhem Land came in for a splendid haul. They ate them.'

'Oh ... What a tragic story, for in addition to all

those deaths, the owner lost his cattle.'

'All part of the difficulties at that time, Gail. People don't seem to realize just what the first men and women went through in paving the way for the fortunates like me.'

She looked swiftly at him, admiration strong within her at his free admission that he was fortunate, and that he was ever aware of the fact that people had died so that the country could be what it now was, productive even though it was often termed a wilderness by those who found its loneliness and harsh austerity unbearable.

'I expect there are numerous stories of similar hardships,' she said at length.

'Too numerous to relate,' he returned. 'Men have wandered, delirious because of thirst and heat, and then dropped, to be buried by comrades who themselves were almost dead. Some were slain by the hostile Abos, some went mad owing to the solitude – especially a station manager who lived entirely alone. It's a strange thing,' he continued, his voice and expression grave and faintly sad, 'that people of high intellect can suffer an inversion of character under conditions that prevail out here. There's a threat in the evil of isolation, a threat to a man's sanity.'

She nodded in agreement, musing on the way in which she herself had wanted to come out here. But she was not alone, nor very far from that gay gathering or the homestead or bungalows. She tried to imagine herself out here alone – no, out there, tramping that void that had no direction, no landmark for guidance ... and no water that was visible ... She shuddered and Kane turned his head, bringing his gaze from the light of a fire which glowed a very long way off, telling of men in the darkness making billy tea and damper, gathered as they were around a bore-trough.

'What is it, dear?'

'Dear?' She started, wondering if that word had merely slipped out or if Kane had meant to say it.

'I was thinking of what it must be like to be out there, all alone, and just wandering round and round in circles, or perhaps even going forward all the time, getting farther and farther away from the homestead.' Again she shuddered and to her utter amazement she felt the comforting touch of Kane's arm about her shoulders.

'That's just how it is,' he returned, and she knew that he refrained from speaking soothing words simply because he wanted nothing more than to bring right home to her the dangers involved in venturing out alone. 'You do go farther and farther away from the homestead – and you can do this just as easily in the daytime as at night,' he added.

'I shall never venture out alone,' she promised. 'I'd never be so foolish as to believe that I could find my way back.'

He told her what happened when anyone was lost in the bush. Every spare man for miles around was put on the hunt.

'Aeroplanes have to be brought into use as well, and the utilities and overlanding cars – everything on wheels, this in addition to the men who search around closer to the homestead; they're on foot, having a deep knowledge of the terrain and also having landmarks which the uninitiated could never hope to pick out.' He looked away swiftly, diverted, and, following the direction of his gaze, Gail gave a gasp of delight and admiration.

'A brumby – see how it seems to quiver in the moonlight!'

He smiled down at her.

'You haven't seen one before?'

'Yes, as a matter of fact I have. But this one's a real picture! I'd love to ride a horse like that.'

'Do you ride, Gail?'

'A little. We hadn't the money when I was very young. I'm glad that Leta is learning already.'

'Dave tells me he's entering her in the gymkhana.'

She glanced up, frowning.

'You don't seem to mind that he's taken her over, as it were?'

'If she's happy and he's happy who am I to interfere?'

She gasped at this indifference, concerning as it did the activities of his own daughter.

'Kane,' she faltered, 'you do love her, don't you?'

He frowned at this and made no immediate answer to her question. When at length he did answer his voice was definitely guarded.

'It's not easy to love someone you haven't known before. I expect I shall learn to love her eventually,' he added, noting Gail's frown, and the way it was deepening.

'When the time comes for you to take her in hand. Then you might love her – if she improves, that is.'

'Don't you believe that she has improved?'

'Yes, a little. Dave can do anything with her.'

'He's always had a way with kids. Pity he hasn't married.' He appeared to be reminded of something, for his expression underwent a change. 'You said that you were coming to like him, if I remember?'

She coloured delicately, profoundly conscious of his piercing regard.

'Nothing could come of it,' she replied, turning her face away in order to conceal her expression. The question which had been hovering in her subconscious leapt right out now and she could not avoid an answer.

She was in love with Kane, the man whom she had

vowed to hate, the man whom she had fully intended should accept the responsibility for his child. Her conscience smiting her, Gail could think only of Sandra, and wonder what she would think were she to know that her cousin had also fallen under the spell of this handsome but arrogant member of the squatocracy.

'I am so ashamed,' she murmured, but silently. 'I only hope that it won't be too long before I can leave here.'

And yet she had no desire now to leave. Had it not been for her parents she felt she would have considered finding herself a post as home help, going far away so that Kane's friends would not hear of what she had done. She could have gone into the sheep-rearing country— Gail cut her musings, realizing that they were just a waste of time.

'Nothing could come of it . . .' Kane was murmuring to himself, and she looked at him. 'Would you like something to come of it?' he asked, and Gail shook her head at once.

'No, I'm not likely to fall in love with Dave.'

He lifted his head slightly – she had the impression that he was relieved to hear her words. Well, naturally he'd be relieved, she decided. It would be a disastrous complication were she to wish to marry Dave! This was what was passing through his mind, she told herself . . . and yet . . . His expression at this moment was very strange indeed—

'Gail dear—' And before she knew what he was intending he had caught her to him and kissed her hard on the mouth. She resisted by instinct, but only fleetingly. This was too delightful, this moment of sheer undiluted magic, and she gladly surrendered her lips when, after the first hard possessive kiss, his lips on hers became more gentle – and persuasive.

'Kane . . . I—' But his release of her lips had been

only momentary and now he was claiming them again, claiming them in a sort of arrogant and masterful way. She felt the pressure of his body against hers; the very warmth of it penetrated, excitingly, temptingly.

'Lovely Gail,' he murmured, his lips close to her cheek. 'My beautiful wife. How could we have parted like that? Why didn't you come to me sooner?' He held her very close and when in her bewilderment she would have spoken her words were cut on the instant by the pressure of his lips on hers. 'Be quiet,' he hissed. 'We're being watched from among those bushes — Rachel!'

'Rachel,' she repeated, her voice husky with shame and disillusionment. It was all an act, put on because his stepmother was spying, trying to discover something by watching them when they were quite alone.

'Yes,' he whispered, 'Rachel. Let's give her some more, shall we?' Amusement in his tones now and Gail felt she must run from him, run to the privacy of her room and recover from this shock. But even had she tried she would not have got very far. 'I hope you don't mind—?' He was actually laughing, silently, for his shoulders shook. 'Sweetheart, don't ever let us part again. And our darling Leta — we must remain together always, so that she'll grow up having both mother and father.' He paused and commanded in a whisper, 'Say something, Gail!'

She swallowed, but her throat was so dry that it hurt. However, she did manage presently to say,

'Yes, dearest Kane, we must stay together always . . .' But her voice trailed away to silence and she brushed a hand across her cheek, removing the tear that had fallen. 'Kane,' she whispered huskily, 'please let's go back.'

'Shall we go back, my love?' he suggested in a tone that could be heard by the woman in the bushes. 'You can't stay too long away from your guests.' He took her hand 'Come, darling,' he said, and the next moment they were on their way to rejoin the happy throng who were dancing to music relayed through two large speakers fixed to the wall of the shed.

If only she could escape, Gail was thinking when eventually they reached the verandah. Kane excused himself and went off to talk to an elderly couple who were sitting at a table at the far end of the verandah, eating refreshments. But escape was impossible since it was her party. Bitterly she reflected on her anticipation of this night ... and that attention she had been given by the man whose wife she was supposed to be. Fool that she was, revelling in something that from the very first was nothing more than an act – and she had known it was an act, so there was no use blaming Kane. But that scene out there in the bush ... Yes, she did blame him! He should have warned first and made advances afterwards. It was totally unfair of him to have kissed her, especially in the way he had kissed her. For that had not seemed in any way to be an act. Those kisses had been so real that it was no wonder she was deceived.

'Gail!' It was Dave who came up to her as she entered the shed proper. 'I want you to meet Georgina.' And with a guiding hand on her arm Dave brought forward a pretty girl with golden hair and large hazel eyes. Slim, and dressed in a full-length velvet skirt and frilly lace blouse, she made as charming a picture as any man could desire. Dave was obviously in his element – looking happier than Gail had ever seen him. Having made the introductions, watched by several graziers who were seated at a nearby table, Dave suggested they should go outside to sit in the fresh air. But, aware that her inclusion was made merely for politeness, Gail made an excuse and allowed the couple to go off on their own.

As there was no one to whom she could talk just at that moment Gail wandered off on her own into the garden, making her exit by a low window so that Dave and his companion should not see her. She felt utterly lost and dejected. And she squirmed with embarrassment at the memory of her eager reciprocation to Kane's kisses. But after some considerable thought, she reached the conclusion that he himself had not taken in the fact of this response. And only then did she feel less tensed and ashamed. If he had not noticed then she would have no difficulty in facing him tomorrow, in the cold light of day. Of course, she and he would come into contact again tonight, but perhaps only briefly, for the party was fast drawing to its close, the time being almost one o'clock in the morning.

She had turned to retrace her steps when she stopped in her tracks on hearing the low and questioning voice of Rachel who, it would seem, was talking to someone, and both she and this other person were screened by a rustic trellis covered by a bougainvillaea vine.

'But you were in England at that time, Joseph. Surely you and he would have discussed your visits?'

'I just went straight there, whereas Kane toured Europe.'

'I don't believe he toured Europe at all! He isn't the one to leave his work!'

'He did, Mrs. Farrell,' insisted the man who, Gail thought, sounded as if he would escape if he could. 'I know he did, because he showed his slides one night at a barbecue which he gave — that was long before you came, of course—'

'Go on,' interrupted Rachel urgently. 'All right, he toured Europe — but did he go to England, that's what I'm trying to find out!'

'He must have. The young Mrs. Farrell—'

'All right, all right! You either don't know anything or else you're determined not to talk. But remember,' she added in a threatening and rasping voice, 'what I've said! If you so much as let out a murmur about this conversation I shan't hesitate to expose your affair with the wife of your employer – the boss of Wolton Creek Station! And now you can get back to your lady love,' she added with a sneer. 'She'll be hunting for you – wondering where you are.'

Gail stood, her heart beating so rapidly that she felt sure it must be heard by the two behind the trellis, and waited for them to come out and find her here; but to her inordinate relief they both went the other way and she was free to walk on unseen by either of them.

Kane found her sitting by the pool, her chin in her hands. She was crying, and in some consternation she tried to keep her face averted. But he tilted it up with a gentle finger under her chin.

'Why are you crying?' he wanted to know, his grey eyes searching her face as if they would find an answer there. 'My dear—'

'It's Rachel,' she broke in desperately, her one intention being to keep from him the real reason for her tears. 'Kane, she's been trying to extract information from someone – no, don't ask me his name,' she added hurriedly, even though Kane had not made any attempt to do so. 'I won't divulge it – or what the hold over him was. But—'

'Gail dear,' broke in Kane gently, 'you're not being at all clear. See, I shall sit down here beside you, and you shall tell me everything.'

'It's Rachel—'

'On second thoughts,' he interrupted, 'I feel it will be better to find some spot which is more private. My stepmother seems to be far too active tonight for me to take any risks. Come—' He took her trembling hand

168

and helped her to her feet. 'We'll go into the house and talk.'

CHAPTER TEN

By the time they had reached the homestead Gail had managed to gain command of her emotions sufficiently for her to relate most of what she had heard. Kane listening intently, appeared to be as deeply interested in her as he was in the story she was telling. His expression was curious indeed, yet unreadable. He had complete control of any emotions that her story might have aroused within him, and this surprised her, expecting as she was a swift show of anger.

'She suspects — and that's a pity, because, as I told you earlier, I rather thought we were to get rid of her.'

'We . . .' A turn of phrase only; it did not mean a thing. Gail's lip quivered, but she averted her head so that he would not see.

'Do you think something happened this evening — something which aroused her suspicions?' she managed to inquire presently.

'Her suspicions were aroused some time ago — in fact, they were probably there all the time, since the day I produced, in so dramatic a manner, my long-lost wife and child.' He spoke almost casually, just as if he was not too perturbed at all by these suspicions which his stepmother had. 'But there was nothing she could do about it — she could scarcely tell me to my face that I was tricking her, and that you and Leta were not my wife and child.'

'No . . .' Gail was thoughtful. 'I do realize that she's had these suspicions — her questions to me that time proved it. However, as you say, there was nothing she could do, and so she was, you think, ready to accept the inevitable and make her exit. But twice this evening she's been trying to find things out—'

'Her watching us was intended,' he broke in, his brow furrowed in thought. 'That's why she didn't appear at the party. Her intention was to have me believe that she and Ertha were staying at home. I wonder what Ertha's been up to this evening?' he added as an afterthought.

He little realized just how soon he was to find out! For he and Gail had been talking only a mere five minutes or so when the door opened without even a knock and Ertha and her mother entered the room. Kane's eyes smouldered as, standing up, he demanded to know the meaning of so unceremonious an entry into his private sitting-room.

'I have some important things to say to you,' began his stepmother, but she was interrupted and told that they were not so important that they could not be left until tomorrow.

'The time's almost two o'clock! I have no intention of talking to you until—'

'I think,' cut in Ertha, her tones cold as ice, 'that you will listen, now! Otherwise, Kane— No! Allow me to speak! Otherwise you're going to find yourself denounced before your guests. I believe the house will be full in a few minutes when they all appear – those who are staying, that is!' Ertha's face was pale with anger; the glance she threw at Gail was alive with venom. Mrs. Farrell, having seated herself, was looking rather worn, and Gail did not wonder at it, since she had been outside, probably all the evening, wandering about, searching for an opportunity of spying on her stepson and his 'wife'.

'I see . . .' So quiet the tone, and, to Gail's alert ears, resigned. 'Carry on, then; let's have it all.' Kane sat down again and leant back, languidly, against the upholstery, his piercing eyes fixed intently on Ertha's face.

Gail too, was watching her and, fascinated, she saw the girl bring a picture book from behind her back.

'What—!' exclaimed Gail, instantly recognizing the book. 'That belongs to Leta.'

'So I assumed. I might as well come straight to the point, Kane,' said Ertha, turning to him but idly flicking back the cover of the book. 'I've been into Leta's playroom this evening – the opportunity of doing so being afforded me by the absence from the house of any prying eyes—' She sent Gail a glance of utter contempt. 'I found this book ...' Slow deliberate words that sent an involuntary shiver down Gail's spine. She knew what was coming next and her eyes sought those of Kane, sending out her apology in advance, but to her amazement he was smiling and his attitude was still one of languid comfort as he rested his back against the chair, 'The child's name is here, inside the cover. Her name is Leta Stafford.'

The final, dramatic sentence was almost spat out, but rang with triumph all the same. Gail, scarcely knowing what she was saying, so put out was she by this discovery, suggested that the book was one that had been lent to Leta by a friend, and it had not been returned before they left England. But even as the words left her lips she realized just how weak they must sound. Kane thought the same, because when she lifted her face to look at him he was shaking his head from side to side as if to say, 'It won't do, Gail.' But he was retaining his calm exterior and she did wish she could do the same. She was hot and flustered and feeling defeated in addition to the unhappiness she was experiencing as a result of what had happened out there in the bush. And she was desperately tired into the bargain, so it was no wonder that an ache of tears was troubling her and causing her to blink rapidly in order to keep those tears from falling. She glanced again at Kane, sending him another apology and silently pleading with him to overlook her lack of foresight in leaving the book around.

Ertha was speaking, saying softly, and with a hint of amused contempt in her voice,

'You mean she had a friend called Leta?' A short laugh and then, 'You're not very clever at thinking up excuses, are you? Leta . . . A name so uncommon that I haven't even heard of it before, and yet she had a friend of the same name. What a remarkable coincidence!'

Kane spoke at last, his grey eyes narrowed almost to slits.

'Just what are you trying to prove?' he asked in his unhurried Australian drawl. 'Cut out the procrastination.'

She looked directly at him and said,

'This woman here is not your wife!'

Silence, the silence of tension, the very air seemed to vibrate with it.

'And so,' came in Mrs. Farrell at last, 'I shall not be leaving here. On the contrary,' she added, managing to sit up straight as an illustration of her authority, 'I shall from tomorrow be resuming my position as mistress here.'

'I think not, Rachel.'

'Oh, and what makes you say that?' Was she in doubt? wondered Gail. Her face had gone pale and her hands, clasped together in her lap, were tightening so that the knuckle bones shone through the skin. 'That autocratic, superior manner won't serve you this time, Kane.' Mrs. Farrell looked to her daughter for support and Ertha responded with the information that she had been into Gail's room too, and examined her passport and other documents.

'There is no doubt whatsoever that her name's Stafford,' she asserted, poison in her tone.

'You've been prying into my private papers!' Gail could scarcely believe what she had heard. 'You despicable creature!' It was her turn to exhibit contempt and this she did, her eyes wandering from the girl's face to her feet and back again. 'I don't know how you dare own to such disgusting conduct!' Aware that Kane was watching her with keen interest, Gail flushed and lowered her head. But he was amused, as she discovered from his laugh as he said,

'What an entertaining little scene this is.'

'You think so?' sneered his stepmother. 'We'll see whether you're as pleasantly entertained by the next part of it.'

'You have something else – er – up your sleeve, Rachel?'

'I want this wanton and the brat Leta sending away! You'll make the promise here and now – otherwise you'll be denounced—' Mrs. Farrell stopped speaking and cocked an ear. 'The first of your guests have come in,' she told him unnecessarily. 'The promise, or else!' And when he made no attempt to answer, 'This will be more than a nine days' wonder, Kane. You have an illegitimate child, remember! That in itself is going to bring your name right down into the mud! Make your decision, because you haven't much time!'

'So it would appear,' agreed Kane, lifting a hand to stifle a yawn.

Momentarily at a loss, Mrs. Farrell turned her attention to Gail.

'You,' she said imperiously. 'Are you willing to be shown up in front of all those people? I make no idle threats, girl! I shall speak right out and say that your child is illegitimate—'

'That's enough!' Kane stood up and the three women all started at the white-hot fury that mingled with the deep bronze of the sun-bitten skin. 'That is slander! Gail doesn't happen to have a child – any child – get that!'

Gail could only stare, her heart throbbing so that the pain was very close to being physical. For there was no doubt at all that Kane was possessed of a searing fury and that fury was all on her account!

'What are you talking about?' Ertha's face had gone a sickly green. 'Leta's her child – and yours—' But she stepped back before she had finished, since Kane had come towards her as if he meant to strike her across the mouth.

'Leta is not her child! By God, Ertha, you're asking for it! Apologize to Gail at once!'

'But—'

'I said apologize, and then get out of here!'

'Look here, Kane—' began Mrs. Farrell, but she was also prevented from continuing as Kane ordered her out of the room.

'If you're not gone in ten seconds I shall throw you out bodily!'

Gail gasped at this threat which, judging from his expression, he would not hesitate to carry out. His fury was unbelievable and she was heartily thankful that she was not the cause of it.

'I'll go—' Mrs. Farrell rose in a hurry as she saw his sudden movement towards her. 'But I shall denounce you—'

'Denounce away – and see where it gets you!'

She left the room without a backward glance and as the door closed behind her Kane once again ordered Ertha to apologize to Gail. A long hesitation followed but, aware now that something was drastically wrong, the girl obeyed, although her apology was spoken in tones of snake-like virulence.

'Kane,' said Gail rather breathlessly as Ertha left the room, 'what is all this about? I mean, you don't seem at all perturbed that they're going to denounce you.' She stopped, her heart seeming to turn a somersault as she noted his expression. 'Kane—' She got no further, for, coming to her, he took her hands in his and said quietly,

'Gail – dear Gail, will you marry me?'

'Marry . . .?' Despite what was so plainly written into his expression she was dazed by the question. And because she just stood there, staring up at him, he jumped to a wrong conclusion and promptly assured her that he was not asking her to marry him simply to thwart Rachel.

'She's found out the truth and she could denounce me; she would also remain here if you went. But that's not my reason for wanting to marry you.' He smiled lovingly at her and once again her heart did strange things. 'Out there, this evening, I discovered that I loved you—'

'Oh, but no, you didn't!' she interrupted without thinking. 'It was an act. You said it was.' A catch in her voice told its own tale of the hurt she had received, and tenderly he drew her to him and kissed her unresisting lips. 'You did say it was,' she repeated when at length he had released her.

'And that was true. There in the shadows I saw Rachel – no one could possibly mistake that shape! Well, I wanted only to give her something convincing, and that was why I acted as I did.' He stopped and smiled ruefully down at her. 'Dearest Gail, it was when I kissed you that I at last owned that you were the girl for me.'

'At last?' in some puzzlement, and then she was hearing that Kane had been noticing her as a woman for some time.

'But only a fortnight ago you reminded me that I was only an employee and that I would soon be leaving here.'

'I did.' He frowned a little. 'You see, marriage had not appealed much to me, and I must admit that I had no wish to be involved in any intimate relationship.' Again he paused and Gail recalled that Dave had said some such thing about the Boss of Vernay Downs. 'However, since that evening I have been gradually accepting the fact that you appeal to me and tonight I knew that my bachelor days were rapidly coming to an end.'

She looked at him, deliriously happy, but yet into her happiness there intruded the picture of Sandra.

'Kane,' she said, and in her voice was a plea. 'Sandra . . . you must have told her that you loved her . . .?'

Silence. Gail's heart was no longer light, nor were her eyes. Yet she offered no resistance when Kane once again drew her close to his breast and, lifting her face, kissed her tenderly on the lips. And then, ignoring her reference to Sandra, he said with a hint of amusement,

'You haven't asked me how I know that you love me – oh, yes, I know it! I discovered it this evening when you responded so delightfully to my kisses. That's why I could ask you to marry me; I was confident that you would answer yes.'

His words thrilled her and yet she could not fully appreciate them at this particular time.

'Sandra,' she murmured. 'And Leta . . .?'

'Remember those "parts unknown"?' he asked, and, when she nodded her head, 'you're shortly going to know what they are.' A glance at his watch and then, 'I hear laughter and chatter, so it would appear that our guests are not too tired to listen to a bedtime story.

Come, my love, and we'll see that they're further entertained.' Lightheartedly he kissed her, ignoring her perplexed look and slight frown of censure. 'Patience, my child— Oh, by the way, although I do know the answer to my question I should very much like to hear it.'

She blushed adorably, and because she was sure now that there had been a great mistake regarding Kane and Sandra, she gave him the answer in soft and loving tones.

'Yes, Kane, I will marry you,' and she added, because she just could not help it, 'I love you dearly . . .' But her voice trailed off to silence because of his amused smile and because of her own shyness, and because her heart was really too full for words.

And so she asked no questions as, holding her by the hand, Kane took her along to the gracious lounge where some of the guests were either sitting or standing around, chatting in little groups. Others had not yet come in; they would talk for a long while yet, standing by their utilities or overlanding cars, for a party like this was always an occasion for staying out until the early hours of the morning. But eventually they would drive away, to tackle distances from fifty miles to perhaps a couple of hundred. Only those whose stations were further away than that would be staying the night.

A silence fell on the room as Kane and Gail entered, but almost immediately it was broken as one grazier after another offered thanks for the wonderful party which Kane had put on for them. But he raised a hand, as he stood there, framed in the open doorway, Gail's hand still clasped in his strong brown fingers. It was a tense moment as the hush fell upon the room; all appeared to be arrested by their host's expression and on each face was a look of expectancy. Gail, feeling she needed support, freed her hand and sat down in a chair not far from where Kane was standing. Her heart was beating too fast for comfort and she wished the next few minutes were over, as she was still bewildered by all that was unknown to her, bewildered because, even now, she was a tiny bit afraid of her doubts. Her eyes, like his, moved over the men and women gathered in the lovely room. The women were as well dressed as any Gail had seen, and their husbands too – these sun-tanned men of the wide open spaces, self-reliant and tough, good-natured and friendly. She liked them all and felt proud to think that she would soon be calling them her friends.

'Firstly,' began Kane, as coolly as if he was an experienced professor preparing to give a lecture to his students, 'I must thank you all for coming, and also for your appreciation – which you have just mentioned, and which was quite unnecessary.' He spoke graciously, sparing a swift glance for Gail. She smiled and he responded before turning his head again and looking at his guests. 'And now,' he continued, 'I have a strange story to tell. It won't take too long, my friends, but I feel that you'll find it interesting despite its brevity.' He paused, but not a sound was heard – and only one person moved. That was Dave. He seemed to be uncertain whether he had the right to stay or not. However, he settled down, leaning against the frame of the window and staring with interest at his employer. The story, Kane was saying, began some years previously when a man named Kenneth Farrell came to work at Vernay Downs as a rouseabout.

'He was a tall and handsome man, but his character was not as attractive as his physical appearance. He drank heavily, spending his leaves at Cullungong, drinking until all his money was gone . . .' His voice drew to a slow stop and he glanced expressionlessly at Gail who, having given a start, had attracted his attention.

Kenneth Farrell . . . she was thinking. Kenneth Farrell — a rouseabout . . . Already the first pieces of the puzzle were falling into place. But to her only; the rest of Kane's audience were gazing at him with expressions of keen expectancy not unmingled with perplexity.

'From my father,' continued Kane in his cool efficient way, 'I learned that this man had, since coming to work for him, discovered that he was in fact related to us, and that, two generations back, his branch of the family had lost all because of a disheritance. But, had this disheritance not occurred, this property would have been in the possession of this Kenneth Farrell, and not in the possession of my father at all. Kenneth Farrell from then on became almost vicious in his manner, refusing to take orders or, in fact, to work at all if he didn't feel like it.' Here Kane gave a shrug and Simon Wallis, an elderly grazier who had been a great friend of Kane's father, interposed with the comment that this insolent and idle rouseabout would soon have been sent on his way. Kane nodded his head, saying that this was exactly what had happened.

'But my father heard later that, even when he was working for him, this man would boast — when he'd had too much to drink, that was — that he was the owner of this station. He even assumed the name of Kane.'

'But no one would believe him. Everyone in Cullungong knows both you and your father!' This interruption came from another grazier, a younger man and a firm friend of Kane's.

'Not here — not anywhere in the Outback. But,' continued Kane with a swift glance in Gail's direction, 'this man went to England to visit relatives. This was after he had been working on a sheep station and had obviously been able to save some money in spite of his drinking habits. You will realize that these relatives would also be my relatives — although several times removed.' Heads nodded, but impatiently. For by now everyone was eager for the story to continue. As far as Gail was concerned it was almost completed; the pieces had fallen into place rapidly and only a few were still missing. She did not need to hear Kane's added information that the visit of this man had taken place about five and a half years go. 'During this holiday he met a girl named Sandra Stafford. She fell in love with him and, some months after Farrell had deserted her — coming back here on his own — this girl had a child whom she called Leta—'

'Leta!' The one word came as a chorus, but almost immediately a deep hush fell upon the room again, every eye turned to Gail.

'Before I continue,' said Kane, not without a hint of anger, 'I want you to discard the idea that Sandra and Gail are one and the same girl.'

'Oh . . .' That spoke for itself, and Gail found herself blushing hotly.

'About four and a half years ago a letter arrived addressed to Kane Farrell and I naturally opened it. It told of the birth of the child, and the writer — Sandra Stafford — was asking for help as she wished to keep the child rather than have it adopted or put into care.' He stopped, for now there was an angry murmuring and he was not prepared to raise his voice.

'You mean,' interrupted Simon, 'that this man had told the girl that he owned this property?'

'That is exactly what I mean,' Kane answered, and Gail instantly thought of her impression that Leta's father was a boaster. Here, she thought, was another irksome little matter cleared up, for since coming here and getting to know Kane, she could not for one moment believe that he would boast of his possessions.

'You realized that it was this man Kenneth who was the father?' Simon put the question, a deep frown on his brown and rugged countenance.

'Yes, I did, but as I didn't know where the man was I tossed the letter into the waste-paper basket,' he said, and Gail flinched. Poor Sandra!

'Naturally you put it into the waste-paper basket! It wasn't your affair, much as the poor girl might be suffering hardship!' This time it was Mary Drayford who spoke. She was about Gail's age and the wife of a station manager. 'All the same,' she added with a sudden frown, 'it was a pity you didn't know where this scoundrel was living.'

'When the second letter arrived I did make it my business to have inquiries set afoot, and on the success of these inquiries I sent the letter on to Farrell, informing him that a previous one whose contents were similar had been destroyed by me. I heard nothing . . .' His voice trailed off as Dave made a movement with his hand. 'Yes?'

'Kenneth Farrell was killed by a scrub,' came the information, falling on astounded ears. 'It was just over three years ago — wait . . .' Dave's brow furrowed in concentration. 'It might have been a little before that.'

Kane looked inquiringly at him.

'How do you know this, Dave? You weren't here when Farrell worked for my father.'

Dave, colouring slightly, asked if he might leave his answer until he could speak privately to Kane. Gail stared, had been staring since Dave's unexpected interruption. She heard Kane say quietly,

'Of course, Dave. Perhaps you'll see me later tonight?'

'If that's what you wish.' Dave looked away as Gail continued to stare at him interrogatingly. All the others

182

in the room were plainly disappointed at this part of the story being denied them, but as Kane was beginning to speak again the murmurings came to a stop.

He explained that nothing more had been heard either of the girl or Farrell, but had not progressed very far when someone interrupted to ask if Farrell had married the girl.

'It's not possible at present to say. Gail is Sandra's cousin and it was she who went through her things when she died. No marriage certificate was found and my own opinion is that there never was a marriage—'

'But Sandra always maintained that there had been a marriage,' broke in Gail impulsively, and then apologized for doing so.

'Yes, dear, but personally I feel that she said this merely because she hated the disgrace. She never used the name Farrell either for herself or for her child, you said.'

'Yes, that's quite right.' She paused. 'Shall we ever know?'

'That's what we shall discuss later. There'll be a very simple way of finding out,' he added with a smile, and Gail lapsed once more into silence. However, within a couple of minutes she was making another interruption, asking in the same impulsive way if Kane had been in England at that particular time. Adding that he must have been away from Vernay Downs or otherwise he would not have been able to tell his friends that he was married, in England, at that particular time.

'I was touring Europe,' he answered briefly, and there were several murmured agreements about this.

'You showed us your excellent slides,' said Simon, then added, 'I expect we all took it for granted that you'd visited England – but you didn't, apparently?'

Kane shook his head, and then continued with his narrative, his description of the scene when he had been presented with his daughter – in front of some of his stockmen – producing hoots of laughter and cries of regret from the ladies at not being present to witness such an entertaining scene. Gail, blushing furiously, was asked how she came to have the courage and she replied unthinkingly,

'I didn't know him then. I was so intent on not letting him get away with it that I just marched up to him and said I'd like to present him with his daughter.'

Again there was laughter, and because of it no one seemed to bother much about Kane's confession of what transpired later, as a result of Gail's bringing the child to him. When some comments were eventually made they did not condemn. On the contrary, as everyone present knew what trouble he had had with his stepmother he was not blamed at all.

'It was a splendid idea!' exclaimed one young grazier. 'But has it worked?'

'No,' came a booming female voice as Mrs. Farrell swept into the room, all her tiredness appearing to have disappeared. 'Ertha and I have been standing outside the door and we've heard every word. That woman—' she pointed to Gail, her eyes dark with fury, 'is not staying in this house! Nor is that unmanageable brat with the unknown father—'

'Stop!' To everyone's amazement it was Dave who intervened, his face white with fury. 'Leave Leta's name out of it, damn you!'

'Dave,' admonished Kane softly, 'what on earth's wrong with you, man?'

Everyone was stirring excitedly. Here in the Outback they were used to making their own entertainments, and each grazier would try out something novel at times. But never had an entertainment like this been presented to them!

'Never mind him,' snapped Mrs. Farrell, who was now supported by the presence of her daughter. 'The story was entertaining, Kane, but the end might be disappointing both to some of your friends who haven't said anything very complimentary about me, and to you yourself. You see,' she added, coming close and looking up at him with a triumphant expression, 'I am mistress here and that's the way it stays! You can't bring in a girl you scarcely know and put her in my place—'

'Be quiet, Rachel,' intervened Kane with a pained expression. 'I've said before that you talk without thinking. *I* am the one who will tell the end of the story, not you!' A hush descended once more at this and with a gentle little tug Kane had Gail on her feet, one hand tightly clasped in his. 'My friends,' he said, and now his voice was more husky than usual for he was clearly affected by emotion, 'Gail has tonight consented to be my wife—'

'Your wife? Bravo, Gail! It's time he was caught!'

'Congratulations to you both!'

'But what wonderful news!'

'Did you choose her for her beauty or her courage?'

It went on for a few seconds more, with Dave the only one making no comment and with Mrs Farrell and Ertha sidling through the door, hoping to get away unseen. But Kane cut round and said,

'Well, Rachel, are you now going to accept my offer of a house?'

The woman maintained an obstinate silence, but her daughter, taking her arm, said quietly,

'Yes, Kane, Mother will accept your offer.'

Gail and Kane were sitting on the front verandah,

having come out a few minutes earlier for a sundowner. Into their line of vision appeared two young people, Dave and Georgina, strolling hand in hand. But on seeing the two on the verandah they waved happily and, turning to her fiancé, Gail smiled and gave a small contented sigh.

'Hasn't it all worked out well?' she said dreamily. 'Dave marrying Georgina and their adopting Leta.'

'It's worked out very well,' he agreed. 'But how strange that Dave should have pieced so many scraps together and produced a picture that none of us knew of.'

'He knew we weren't married, of course, he told you that on the night you told your story.' Kane nodded at this unnecessary statement and Gail continued, 'He hadn't connected his second cousin, Kenneth Farrell, with this business until you began talking. And then it all came to him.'

'But he did appear troubled about something even before I began to relate everything, if you remember?'

'It could have been because he knew instinctively that he was going to have to admit that he's known almost from the first that you and I weren't married.'

'Yes, it could,' agreed Kane, and then, changing the subject somewhat, 'It was a good idea to ask Leta what she wanted — before telling Dave and Georgina that they could have her.' Kane paused a moment. 'I had promised to keep her, and as I said when you later asked me — after we were engaged — she could have made her home with us. But for her own happiness it's better that she goes to Dave. He wants her and she chose to live with him when she was offered a choice.'

'So I have nothing to reproach myself for where my

promise to Sandra is concerned. I couldn't bring her to her father, but I've brought her to another relative.'

'You do realize that from all this has emerged the fact that Dave and I are cousins several times removed?'

She nodded, but said nothing. She and Kane had talked a great deal during the past three weeks and everything had been carefully straightened out. They were to be married in a week's time and Gail's parents would be here to give her and Kane their blessing.

'Look at the sunset!' she exclaimed suddenly. 'Oh, Kane, I'm going to love being here.'

He smiled tenderly at her and, rising to his feet, he pulled her up too, and into the protection of his arms. The sun, falling quickly behind the mountains, was painting the sky with bronze and crimson and gold. The summits were on fire. But over the endless bush-lands the glow was softer, burnishing the casuarina trees growing along the watercourse; and away where the billabong shone like a pool of gold the clustered Red River gums cast gentle shadows as their branches were stirred by the breeze blowing down from the mountains. All was silent; all was still over this infinite void which for Gail had such charm and character.

'My darling Gail ...' The tenderly-spoken words brought her from the delights of nature to the even greater delight of her lover's kiss. 'How glad I am that you came to me.'

She said nothing, because of the deep emotion within her heart. It was enough that she drew closer to him, content to be there as, together, they watched the glory of the sunset as it sprayed the endless plains with gold.

Harlequin Plus

A WORD ABOUT THE AUTHOR

Anne Hampson, one of Harlequin's most prolific writers, is the author of more than thirty Romances and thirty Presents. She holds the distinction of having written the first two Harlequin Presents, in 1973: *Gates of Steel* and *Master of Moonrock*.

Anne is also one of Harlequin's most widely traveled authors, her research taking her to ever new and exotic settings. And wherever she goes she takes copious notes, absorbs all she can about the flora and fauna and becomes completely involved with the people and their customs.

Anne taught school for four years before turning to writing full-time. Her outside interests include collecting antiques, rocks and fossils, and travel is one of her greatest pleasures—but only by ship; like many, she's afraid of flying.

What does she like most? "Sparkling streams, clear starry nights, the breeze on my face. Anything, in fact, that has to do with nature."

Harlequin ◆ Salutes...

JANET DAILEY

...with 6 more of her
bestselling Presents novels!

Once again Harlequin is proud to salute Janet Dailey,
one of the world's most popular romance authors. Now's
your chance to discover 6 of Janet Dailey's best—6 great
love stories that will intrigue you, captivate you and
thrill you as only Harlequin romances can!

Available in May wherever paperback books are sold, or through
Harlequin Reader Service:

In the U.S.
1440 South Priest Drive
Tempe, AZ 85281

In Canada
649 Ontario Street
Stratford, Ontario N5A 6W2

FREE!

A hardcover Romance Treasury volume
containing 3 treasured works of romance
by 3 outstanding Harlequin authors...

...as your introduction to Harlequin's
Romance Treasury subscription plan!

Romance Treasury

...almost 600 pages of exciting romance reading
every month at the low cost of $6.97 a volume!

A wonderful way to collect many of Harlequin's most beautiful love
stories, all originally published in the late '60s and early '70s.
Each value-packed volume, bound in a distinctive gold-embossed
leatherette case and wrapped in a colorfully illustrated dust jacket,
contains...
- 3 full-length novels by 3 world-famous authors of romance fiction
- a unique illustration for every novel
- the elegant touch of a delicate bound-in ribbon bookmark...
  and much, much more!

Romance Treasury

...for a library of romance you'll treasure forever!

Complete and mail today the FREE gift certificate and subscription
reservation on the following page.

Romance Treasury

An exciting opportunity to collect treasured works of romance! Almost 600 pages of exciting romance reading in each beautifully bound hardcover volume!

You may cancel your subscription whenever you wish! You don't have to buy any minimum number of volumes. Whenever you decide to stop your subscription just drop us a line and we'll cancel all further shipments.